BRIGHT GIRL

BRIGHT GIRL

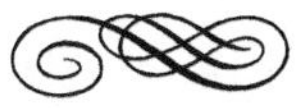

NANCY BASILE

Free Book!

Would you like to peek behind the curtain? Follow my ups and downs, new deals, book sales, giveaways, and more? Sign up for Nancy's Newsletter! https://short.im/newsletter As a special thank you for signing up, you'll receive an exclusive copy of the prequel to my River Sutton Mysteries series, *A Shoulder to Die On*.

Contents

For my mother, who reads everything I write. Thank you for your support and encouragement.

One

Detective Shelby Reed kneeled by the body. With a gloved hand, she swept the girl's long, wavy hair aside to examine the marks around her neck. Bruises and abrasions, indicating she'd been strangled. Too bad. She was pretty, and so young.

Shelby closed the girl's hazel eyes and stood. She scanned the blue-painted cement of the empty swimming pool where the girl had been dumped. Dead leaves littered the ground, along with a candy bar wrapper and an empty potato chip bag. Shallow puddles were full of silt and soggy grass. Nothing revealing. A private hang-out spot for teens.

"Forensics is here, Detective." Officer Naomi Kim nodded to the aluminum ladder they'd put in place, allowing them easy access to the deep end. Two people in protective gear descended the ladder, while another officer lowered a duffel full of equipment using a rope.

"Good." Shelby took several paces away from the body, nodding to the forensics team as they started their examination. "What do we know so far?"

Shelby had been enjoying a quiet morning at home with a cup of black coffee and a fried egg sandwich when she received Naomi's call. She finally had a Saturday off. At first, she was annoyed to be called to a cold, empty pool. But after she saw the girl's body, determination replaced her annoyance. And sadness, but she pushed that away.

Naomi flipped open her small notebook. Her hands shook a little. "Early this morning, we received a call from Whitney Chandler's parents saying she didn't come home last night. She's never been out past her curfew, so her parents went to bed around ten, thinking Whitney would be home soon. When they got up this morning and saw her bed hadn't been slept in, they tried calling her phone, but it went straight to voicemail. They called Skye Stevens, a good friend of Whitney's, but Skye didn't know anything. They also called her boyfriend, Bobby Garza, but he said the last time he saw Whitney was last night at a party and she was headed home."

Shelby glanced at the purple marks on Whitney's neck, a knot twisting in her stomach. "Tell me about the boyfriend." Naomi grew up in Locust Grove, a small town where everyone knew everyone else's business. Shelby had moved there just two months ago from Harrisburg to make a fresh start and to be close to her father. She had hoped for straightforward cases and a slow pace. So much for those aspirations.

Naomi squinted at the gray sky while she talked. "Bobby Garza, senior at Bellmoor Prep School here in Locust Grove. Football player. He's been in a few scrapes over the years, but no record."

The knot in Shelby's stomach pulled tighter. "Scrapes? What scrapes?"

Naomi tilted her head back and forth. "Football players on opposing teams. Trash talk that turns into pushes and shoves. We arrested him once for assault, but the other kid's parents didn't press charges. Said it was just 'boys being boys.'" Naomi rolled her eyes.

Shelby agreed with Naomi's rolled-eyes assessment. She'd known plenty of boys who didn't resort to violence when their tempers flared. "Any assaults on girlfriends?"

Naomi pursed her lips and shook her head. "Not that I know of." She shrugged her shoulder. "He's a big deal in Locust Grove. Star tackle. Looking at a full ride to West Virginia University on a football scholarship."

Shelby bit the inside of her cheek while her breakfast churned in her stomach. Another football player with his eyes on a scholarship that would rescue him from the small pond where he'd been a big fish. She swallowed back bile.

"Do you know her parents?"

"They're good people. I went to school with Whitney's older sister. She lives in Colorado now. We weren't friends, but the family was always real nice."

"No history of abuse?"

Naomi reared back. "Oh, good gravy, no. They're super soft-spoken. You'll see when you meet them." Naomi's eyes went wide. "Oh, gosh. You're going to have to tell them about…" Her voice faded away as her gaze landed on Whitney.

Shelby nodded. "Yes, I will. Worst part of the job." While Naomi absorbed this information, Shelby introduced herself to the forensics team, then said, "Anything preliminary you can tell me?"

A man took off his safety goggles. "I'm sure you guessed she was strangled." After Shelby nodded, he continued. "From the front. Broken blood vessels in the eyes, internal damage."

"Woman or man?" Shelby asked.

The man narrowed his eyes. "Probably a man. The spread of the bruises indicates big hands. And there wasn't much of a struggle, so he was pretty strong."

"From the front, you said. To get that close, with little to no struggle, probably someone she knew?"

"Likely," he said. "We pulled small fibers from under her fingernails, but no skin or hair. No DNA."

"Fibers?" Shelby cocked her head. "Tell me about those."

He reached his hand toward his colleague, who handed him a small plastic bag. He held it up for Shelby to inspect. "You can barely see them, but they're red. I'll have to take them back to the lab, but my first guess is synthetic, like polyester or nylon."

"From a jacket, perhaps?"

"Maybe."

"Any prints?"

"Nope." His eyes raked over the body. "She also didn't have a purse or a wallet or even a phone."

"No phone?" Shelby was surprised. Teenagers were almost surgically attached to their phones.

"Not that we could find. Killer could have taken everything."

Shelby nodded. "What about prints on the fence? Or the gate?" A chain-link fence ran around the pool property. When they arrived, the gate was already open. Shelby had noticed, however, that the lock was rusted through. Anyone could have gotten inside.

"Nope. In fact, the gate was wiped." He handed the bag back to his colleague, who was packing up. "I'll keep you posted on those fibers."

"And what you find in her room. I'm assuming you're headed to the Chandlers' next?"

"That's the plan."

"Thanks," she said, watching the other forensics officer tuck Whitney's hair into a body bag before zipping it up. "Please do."

She called to Naomi and the two women climbed the ladder out of the pool. Shelby walked several yards away from the crime scene, the morning breeze lifting her hair. The locust trees, for which the town was named, were golden yellow against the steely sky. She studied the surrounding area while Naomi scribbled in her notebook. Security cameras hung on the brick pool house and on a telephone pole.

"Officer Kim, see if you can get footage from those security cameras from last night."

Naomi wrinkled her nose. "I'll try, Detective, but Joey Bianchi owns the pool. It's been in his family for three generations. I know for a fact they only turn them on during the summer, when the pool's open."

Shelby frowned. "Lax security practices aside, how do you know that 'for a fact?'"

Naomi's cheeks turned pink. "I'd rather not say, Detective."

Although she didn't want to embarrass Naomi, she needed information. "Naomi, if it's of personal nature, your secret is safe with me."

Naomi's blush deepened, but she took a deep breath and said, "Joey's younger brother talked me into making out in the empty pool one time. It was April, and I was worried about getting caught. But he told me no one could see us from ground level and that the cameras were off since it wasn't summer." Her eyes dropped to the ground.

Shelby pressed a knuckle to her mouth to keep from smiling. She studied the few homes that bordered to pool property. "Make a note to canvass the neighbors, see if any of them have Ring doorbells or security cameras."

Naomi scratched a note in her notebook. "Yes, Detective."

Shelby leaned toward Naomi. "So, was it worth the risk?"

Naomi's eyebrows pinched together. "Was what worth the risk, Detective?"

Shelby elbowed her. "Making out with Joey's younger brother."

Naomi's eyes became big as saucers, but then a mischievous grin split her face. "So worth it." She frowned. "Detective, I heard that guy talking about red fibers. Bellmoor's team colors are red and white. Do you think—"

"No theories right now. We're collecting facts and evidence right now, Officer." Shelby disliked being abrupt, but wanted to nip speculation in the bud, especially about football players. Hands on hips, she said, "Okay, Officer. It's time to inform the parents. Maybe they'll have some insight into what happened. Although, if Whitney was like most teenagers, there's a lot they probably don't know."

Shelby and Naomi left the crime scene in their own vehicles to meet up at the station and drive together to the Chandlers' home. Shelby used the brief time to process the information from the scene and to reinforce the mental wall she built between her personal feelings and her professional life. The Chandlers would be devastated, but she could allow herself only so much empathy. She needed a clear head.

Locust Grove was aflame with autumn colors. She'd moved to the small town to escape the scrutiny of the public eye and to be closer to her father, the only family she had left. Both Locust Grove and her father were turning out to be disappointments.

Shelby arrived at the station and waited for Naomi. The young officer climbed into the passenger seat. Her hand shook as she buckled her seatbelt.

Shelby remembered the first time she delivered the worst news a person could hear. She rested her hand on Naomi's shoulder. "Courage, Officer. For Whitney."

Naomi gave her a small smile and nodded. "Courage, Detective."

Two

Shelby watched Jeremy and Lisa Chandler quietly fall apart on their floral upholstered couch. Lisa hid her face in the crook of Jeremy's neck, but her body trembled with sobs. Silent tears fell from Jeremy's eyes as he stared into the distance, holding his wife. Their grief took Shelby right back to the worst day of her life. She understood their shock all too well.

"Mr. and Mrs. Chandler, when was the last time you saw Whitney?"

"After dinner, about six o'clock," Jeremy said. He wiped his cheek on his shoulder, which was covered in a maroon flannel shirt. "Her friend, Skye, picked her up to go to the football game."

Naomi, her lips pressed into a line, kept her eyes on her notebook as they spoke. Shelby felt like she was watching Naomi begin to harden her heart against the horrors of their job. She wished it wasn't necessary, but in the end, Naomi would be better for it.

"Did she text or call any time after that?"

Lisa pulled her face from her husband's neck, dabbing at her puffy face with a well-used tissue. "Just once, to tell us she was going to a party after the game."

"About what time was that and where was the party?"

Lisa sniffed. "She texted us around nine-thirty. And I think the party was at Bobby's."

"Bobby was her boyfriend?" Her guts squirmed just mentioning the football player.

"Yes."

"And you didn't hear from her or see her after that?"

"No." Lisa shook her head. "We watched the nightly news, then went to bed." Her chest heaved.

"Was it your habit not to wait up for her when Whitney was out?" The Chandlers blanched, but Shelby was quick to add, "I'm not judging." She shared a soft smile. "I'm not a parent myself. But I'm wondering if Whitney knew you'd be asleep, based on previous experience."

"Most likely," Jeremy answered. "It was a typical Friday night. Football game, then get together with friends." He swallowed. "She's a good girl. We've never had to worry..." A sob choked off his words.

Shelby nodded. "You've never had to worry because she usually comes home by curfew?"

"We've never needed a curfew with Whitney," Lisa said. "She just naturally came home by midnight, knowing we don't like her out on the roads late at night." Her eyes dropped to her hands, her tissue falling apart. "A lot of drunks on the road."

"Mr. and Mrs. Chandler, do you have any idea who Whitney met at the pool last night?"

Lisa shook her head. "Not a clue. It wouldn't have been Bobby, because she was at his house."

Jeremy rested his hand on his wife's. "And Skye told us this morning that she came home around eleven last night. She didn't stay at the party very long."

"How was Whitney supposed to get home if Skye was her ride?"

"Bobby," Jeremy said. "He would have brought her home. Have you talked to him?" Jeremy's bloodshot stared into hers.

"No. We wanted to come to you first."

He nodded, his eyes glazing over, while Lisa's chin trembled from the effort of holding in her emotions.

"What was Whitney's relationship with Bobby like? How long were they dating?" Shelby clamped down on the flurry of anxiety she felt in her chest.

"They've been dating about a year," Lisa said. "Started last fall, when they were juniors."

Jeremy shrugged. "I know Bobby's been in trouble a few times, but he always treated Whitney real well. Holding doors, giving her little gifts, very respectful. He treated her like she was special. She was special. Such a bright girl." Jeremy covered his face with a hand while he silently shook. Lisa wrapped her arms around him, nestling her face in the crook of his shoulder again.

"I'm almost done with my questions, Mr. and Mrs. Chandler. I appreciate your willingness to talk with me in such a difficult time."

Jeremy gave a loud sniff and lifted his pale face. "Whatever helps you find out who did this to our baby girl." Lisa nodded.

"Like I said," Shelby glanced at each of them. "I appreciate it. Now, we didn't find a purse or wallet or anything on Whitney. Did she take anything with her last night?"

"She has a wristlet purse she always carries," Lisa said, holding up her own wrist to demonstrate. "It was big enough for her phone, her I.D., and some cash or a credit card. It's Vera Bradley. She just had to have one, so she saved up for it." Lisa gave Shelby a watery smile.

"Would she have left it in her locker at school?"

Mrs. Chandler frowned. "No, because then it would be locked up all weekend."

Shelby clasped her hands in her lap. "Mr. and Mrs. Chandler, this is a difficult question to ask, but I have to. Can you think of anyone who had a beef with Whitney? Someone she argued with, maybe? An old boyfriend? A bully?"

Jeremy shook his head. "No. Everyone loved Whitney. She was on track to be valedictorian. Last year, she was on homecoming court, probably would have been this year, too." He gulped back a sob and pressed his fist to his mouth.

Shelby stood from her chair, and Naomi did the same. "Thank you, Mr. and Mrs. Chandler." She removed a business card from her front pocket. "Here's my card with my direct phone number. Call me if you think of anything, anything at all, that might help with our investigation. Again, I'm so sorry for your loss."

Back in her car, Shelby and Naomi stared at the one-story brick house. The Chandlers lived in a middle income neighborhood where everyone had fall wreaths on their doors and kept their lawns neat. In Shelby's experience, neighborhoods like this one held more secrets than most people suspected.

"We'll need to question Bobby next," Shelby said to Naomi. "And Skye. And probably the school principal. He would know more about any enemies Whitney might have had. Do you know Skye's last name?"

"Stevens," Naomi replied as she took more notes. She opened her mouth to say something, but closed it again.

"Go ahead. What were you going to say?"

Naomi squinted at the Chandlers' home through the windshield. "I thought it was interesting that Whitney was friends with Skye, close enough friends that she picked up Whitney for the game."

"Why's that?"

"Well, we'd have to verify it, but I'm pretty sure Skye is on track to be valedictorian, too. She and Whitney were always competing against each other for the top spot in whatever academic contest was happening at Bellmoor. Whitney would be in the paper one week for winning an award, then Skye would be in it the next. Those two were always neck and neck."

Shelby considered this. "Maybe that's why they were friends. Who else could relate to the work it takes to stay at the top, or the pressure they're under?"

"Maybe." Naomi didn't sound convinced. "I always thought it was a frenemy kind of situation."

"Something to keep in mind, but remember, a man strangled Whitney. A woman's hands are too small to make the marks around her neck." She started the car. "Does Skye have a boyfriend?"

"Don't know."

Shelby pulled out of the Chandlers' driveway. "Let's head back to the station, get caught up on our report, and figure out our next steps." A rumbling sound came from the seat next to her. She glanced at Naomi. "Hungry?"

"Starving." Naomi bent over her forearm. "I rushed out this morning without eating."

"We'll hit a drive-through on our way. Nothing like McDonald's hash browns for brain food."

Three

"So I said, 'I'm sorry, I didn't realize it was her turn.'"

Raucous laughter met Shelby and Naomi when they entered the bullpen at the police station. A sandy-haired man had his hip hitched up on a desk, one leg on the ground, holding court. Officer Will Simon and Captain Maria Guerrero stood around him. Both wore wide smiles as they laughed at the stranger's joke.

"Oh, good. Detective Reed, you're here." Captain Guerrero straightened her blazer as Will returned to his own desk. "I'd like you to meet Detective Jasper Erickson, from the Brooke County sheriff's office."

Detective Erickson stood from the desk. He was tall, over six feet, because he was several inches taller than Shelby, who stood at five nine. His broad shoulders filled out his plaid button-up, which he wore with a burgundy tie. His smile was like an ad for Crest Whitener. He held out a hand to Shelby. "Nice to meet you, Detective Reed." He held a coffee mug in his other hand that said "On the Case" with an illustration of a cat sleeping on a briefcase.

She frowned. "That's my mug."

He froze, his eyebrows lifting. He dropped his outstretched hand to his side. "Oh, uh, didn't realize. Okay if I use it just this once?" Then he winked.

Shelby didn't like winkers. They winked because they thought a wink excused their poor behavior. Winkers were used to getting their way.

Captain Guerrero gently elbowed Shelby. "Detective Reed, play nice. There are plenty of mugs in the office."

Shelby gave her a tight smile. "You're right, Captain. I'm just particularly fond of that mug. My husband gave it to me." A tense silence fell over the room, just as Shelby had hoped. Erickson just kept smiling, clueless. Shelby turned to the captain, but kept her eyes on Detective Erickson. "Why is he here?"

Captain Guerrero cleared her throat. "I asked Detective Erickson to partner with you on the Chandler investigation."

Shelby's eyes focused on the captain. "Why? I have a partner." She gestured at Naomi with her thumb over her shoulder. Naomi started, clearly uncomfortable at being drawn into the conversation.

The captain rested her hands on her hips. "Officer Kim doesn't have the experience Detective Erickson has, and we need experience on this case. I want the investigation to be quick and quiet. None of us want to end up on the national news." She gave Shelby a pointed look.

"National News?" Erickson's head swiveled between the Captain and Shelby, but neither responded.

Shelby said, "I have the experience, and I'd like to share it with Officer Kim. Train her up."

The captain shook her head. "Not this time. When CNN takes notice of us, I want two experienced detectives in the spotlight." Her eyes flicked to Naomi. "No offense, Officer Kim."

Naomi shrugged. "No offense taken, Captain." Her cheeks turned pink when she handed her notebook to Erickson. "Here are my notes so far. I'm sure Detective Reed can fill you in." Then she giggled.

Shelby stared at Naomi. Erickson was a handsome man, but there was no reason her co-workers should turn into schoolgirls. They had jobs to do.

"Thanks, Officer Kim, was it?" Erickson gave her a warm smile, which made Naomi blush even deeper. Shelby sucked her teeth with her tongue. He said, "I'll put everything you took down in the report."

"Hold on," Shelby said, holding up a hand. "This partnership isn't final."

"Oh, yes, it is," the captain said, taking a step back from the desk. "Bring Detective Erickson up to speed and have a report on my desk ASAP. I want this case wrapped up as quickly as possible." With that pronouncement, the captain disappeared into her office.

Erickson looked at Shelby like a dog waiting to play fetch. She sighed and stepped toward her desk. Erickson leaned toward her. "I brought coffee and pastries. They're in the conference room. Could we catch up in there?" His bright white smile appeared again.

Without a word, Shelby took off her jacket, grabbed her stuff, and walked into the conference room. As promised, Erickson had brought coffee and baked goods. Who was this guy? How was he so chipper if he had experience as a cop? This job ground out the optimism and good cheer inside a person. His sunny attitude grated on her nerves.

She filled a cup with hot coffee and took a seat. She and Naomi had just eaten, and she wasn't interested in adding carbs to her day. Erickson, however, refilled his mug, and grabbed a Danish and a napkin. Then he rounded the table to sit across from her. All Shelby could think was he must work out a lot if he regularly eats pastries, because he was trim and muscular. Most cops who ate pastries looked like they did.

Once Erickson was settled, Shelby brought out her notes, telling him everything they'd learned so far. As she talked, she took an occasional drink of coffee, while Erickson devoured his Danish like a starving man. At least he wiped his mouth.

He said, "Right now, off the top of my head, sounds like the boyfriend did it. Especially if he has priors."

"No one pressed charges," Shelby reminded him. "So he doesn't have a record."

"No," he said, chewing his Danish. "But he has prior confrontations that turned physical. I used to play football. After a game, you're tired, sure. But your adrenaline is still pumping. Maybe this Bobby met Whitney for some nighttime fun, away from prying eyes. They got into a fight, and his temper got the best of him. I can easily see that happening."

"Well," Shelby sipped her coffee. "That is one possibility. But it's early in the case and we have more people to interview." She went to stand, but Erickson stayed seated, still eating.

He said, "I don't see any reason to interview anyone other than Bobby at this point. Let's go get him and bring him in for questioning."

Shelby stared at Erickson. "He's a kid. The optics of that are terrible. For all we know, Whitney was out for a nighttime stroll and got mugged. Remember, her purse and her phone are missing."

"Optics?" He shrugged, his eyebrows pulling together. "Who cares about optics? We're here to catch a killer."

"I do." Shelby's hands became fists on the tabletop. "Have you ever been in the national spotlight?"

"No." He wiped his hands on his napkin.

"I have. It's no picnic, especially when there are kids involved. So, I'm going to cover all my bases until I have an actual reason to bring in Bobby." This time, she stood, glaring at Erickson.

"Fine," he said, pushing off the table as he also stood. "This is your show. I'm just the good-looking guest star." He grinned.

Shelby barely restrained her eye roll before putting on her jacket and leaving the conference room. "Officer Simon," she called.

Will rose from his desk chair. "Yes, Detective?"

"Take Officer Carter and canvass the homes surrounding the pool. Ask if they have Ring doorbells or other security cameras focused on that area. If they do, ask if we can get copies. If they need a warrant, take note and we'll get one."

"Got it."

"After that, go to Bellmoor Prep. We need to search Whitney's locker and catalog everything in there."

"Do I need a warrant?"

"Not unless they request one. I'm guessing students sign waivers to their rights when it comes to school property. Schools conduct random locker searches all the time. You shouldn't meet any resistance, but if you do, let me know."

"On it." Will grabbed his coat from the back of his chair and disappeared.

Shelby turned to Erickson, who popped a donut hole into his mouth. Her jaw stiffened. "I'll be waiting in my car."

On her way out, she heard Erickson say, "Sheesh. Is she always like this? I feel bad for her husband."

Then she heard Naomi reply, "Oh, she's not married. Her husband died."

There was a beat of silence, then Erickson said, "How?"

"Let's just say she has a reason to steer clear of Bobby Garza."

Four

Shelby stayed laser-focused on the investigation and vowed that Erickson's cavalier attitude wouldn't rankle her. She didn't know how he made detective without allowing the darkness of crime investigation to dim his shiny attitude. Even before the darkest day of her life, her job had hardened any softness she felt for humankind. Softness was a weakness.

Shelby and Erickson pulled up to Bellmoor Preparatory School. They were interviewing Alfred Wheeler, the principal. Hopefully, he had insider knowledge to share about Whitney's student life, Bobby Garza's altercations, and any other persons of interest they could interview.

Mr. Wheeler had said he was in the office on a Saturday to catch up on work when they called him for an interview. He'd asked if they could meet in his office, and Shelby was happy to do so. She'd never been inside the school and wanted to get a feel of the place where Whitney Chandler had spent her days.

"You said the principal's name is Alfred Wheeler?" Erickson asked as he buzzed to be let in. "As in Al Wheeler, former defensive end for Ohio State?"

Shelby peered through the glass of the front door. The linoleum was shiny enough to see your reflection. The hallway in front of them dead-ended in another set of doors that opened onto what looked like an outdoor eating area. "I don't know. Could be."

"Damn. If I'd known I was meeting Al Wheeler today, I would have done something with my hair." Erickson checked his reflection in the window, running his fingers through his already stylish hair, his blazer stretching over his shoulders and biceps.

Before he could primp any further, a loud buzzer and a click sounded from the doors. Erickson swung the door open, holding it for Shelby. She held the next set of doors for him. He saluted her in thanks.

Principal Wheeler met them at the intersection of two hallways, which formed a T. "Detectives, welcome to Bellmoor Preparatory School. I'm sorry it's for such a terrible reason." He was built a lot like Erickson, tall with broad shoulders, but with a soft belly. He looked like an educator in dress slacks, a button-up, and a cardigan.

They introduced themselves and shook hands with him. He held out his arm, leading them down the hallway to his office, which was larger than Shelby had expected. His desk sat on one side of the room, with two chairs facing it. He led them to a sitting area on the other side of the room, indicating they should sit on the couch. "Can I get you anything? Coffee? Water?"

"No, thank you," Shelby said.

He nodded and sat in an armchair perpendicular to the couch. A row of windows facing the parking lot stretched behind him. The other three walls displayed photos of the principal shaking hands with people or posing with his arms around groups, as well as shelves of trophies, plaques, and two framed jerseys embroidered with his name. One jersey looked weathered, and one looked nearly new.

Erickson pointed to the jerseys on the wall. "I was a big fan of yours when you played for Ohio State. You were the reason I wanted to go there."

Wheeler, smiling, crossed his legs at the knee. "Is that right? What year did you graduate?"

"Oh, I didn't end up going to Ohio State. I played for Pitt."

"Ouch," Wheeler said, laughing.

Shelby said, "So, one of those red and white jerseys is from Ohio State and the other...?" She pointed to the newer-looking jersey.

"When I first took over as principal here at Bellmoor, the football team made me an honorary Bobcat."

"Ah," Erickson said. "The Bellmoor Bobcats. Has a nice ring to it. And it's cool that Bellmoor is the same colors as Ohio State. Stay true to the red and white, am I right?" Erickson held his hand up for a high-five. Wheeler chuckled and met it with a soft tap.

"Erickson," Shelby whispered. "A girl is dead."

Erickson sobered immediately, nodding. "Right. Gotcha." He glanced at Wheeler, who had dropped his eyes to the floor.

"Such a tragedy. So young, and such a bright girl." Wheeler swallowed and pressed his lips together for a moment. "I'll do whatever I can to help you, detectives. The safety of all my students is paramount, on or off campus, twenty-four hours a day. I take my job very seriously. We're a small community, and I feel a connection to these students almost as strong as the connection I feel to my own children."

Shelby asked, "Do your children attend Bellmoor?"

"Yes, they do. My son, Al Jr., is a senior, and my daughter, Hannah, is a junior." He ran a hand over the thin layer of hair on his scalp. "They're going to be devastated when they hear."

"Were they friends with Whitney?"

He gave Shelby a quick smile. "No, but, like I said, small community. They're friendly, if not friends, with everyone at Bellmoor Prep."

Shelby studied the principal. There were purple smudges under his pale blue eyes, and his shoulders were bunched near his ears. He looked braced for an impact. She brought out her notebook and pen. "Where were you last night, Mr. Wheeler?"

He blinked rapidly. "I was attending a conference in Pittsburgh at the William Penn Hotel."

"The conference was still going on a Friday night? Isn't that unusual?"

"I don't know. I don't attend a lot of conferences." He shared a self-conscious smile. "I was at the Innovative Schools Summit with one of my teachers, Tom Long. There was a dinner at the end of the conference on Friday night. We came back this morning."

"Must have gotten up pretty early this morning to make it home and then here—" she gestured around the office, "so early."

He shrugged and chuckled. "We're educators. We're used to early wake-up times."

"And where is Mr. Long? Did you drop him off before coming here?"

"No." He shook his head. "We drove separately."

Shelby raised her eyebrows. "Why's that? Wouldn't it have been easier to car pool? Parking and all that?"

"Probably." He shrugged again. "But Tom wanted to have his own car in case he needed to come home for a night."

Shelby frowned. "Why would he do that?" She felt Erickson shift on the couch next to her.

Wheeler ran his tongue over his lips. "I don't know how much I can say." His eyes darted between Shelby and Erickson.

"Mr. Wheeler. Al." Erickson winked. "We hold anything you say in strict confidence. No locker room talk here." Erickson flashed him a wide grin. Shelby bit the inside of her cheek.

Wheeler nodded. "In that case, Tom and his wife have been having problems. He wanted to have his own car if his wife got squirrelly and wanted him to come home."

"Squirrelly?" Shelby asked.

Wheeler stared at his clasped hands. "If she got insecure about where he was and—" he looked up. "Who he was with."

"Ah," Erickson leaned back in his seat. "Message received."

Wheeler gave him a small smile while Shelby frowned at him.

She turned back to the principal. "And your wife? Was she home with the kids all week?"

He scratched the back of his head. "I'm divorced, Detective. My wife lives in Columbus, Ohio."

"Really?" Erickson's eyebrows lifted. "That must be tough, shuttling your kids back and forth."

"I have primary custody. She sees them for holidays and summer vacations." Wheeler's jaw tightened.

"You were gone for a week. How did your children manage while you were gone?"

He gave her a tight smile. "My son is eighteen and they both drive. They had plenty of food and extra cash, just in case. And--if it reassures you--Tom's wife checked in on them."

"Mr. Wheeler—" Shelby started, but Wheeler interrupted.

"Please, call me Al. Everyone does."

Shelby nodded once, then continued, "What kind of student was Whitney? Did she have friends? Enemies? Had she argued recently with anyone?"

Wheeler ran his hands along the arms of his chair, his eyebrows creasing. "Not at all. Whitney was a model student. She was in a close race for valedictorian, as a matter of fact."

"Sometimes," Erickson said, "the pressure of being the best can bring out the worst in people. Was there anyone Whitney didn't like or had a rivalry with?"

Wheeler thought for a moment, but replied, "No. No one. I mean it when I said she was a model student. Top grades, active in clubs, volunteering."

Erickson said, "She was dating Bobby Garza. Any trouble between them? We know," Erickson gestured between himself and Shelby, "that he was known to scrap."

Wheeler nodded. "Yes, there were a couple of incidents when Bobby took his trash talk too far. You played football, Detective." He and Erickson shared a mischievous look. They practically rubbed elbows. Shelby gritted her teeth. "You know how worked up a boy can get. But Bobby's a good kid. I can't see him hurting Whitney."

"We'll need our forensics team to search Whitney's locker."

Erickson eyed Shelby, then said, "And possibly other lockers as the investigation continues. Will that be a problem?"

Wheeler shook his head. "Not at all. The lockers are school property, and I have no issue opening her locker for your investigation."

"Well, I think those are all the questions we have right now, Mr. Wheeler." Shelby stood, which prompted the men to stand, too.

"Al," Wheeler said.

"Here's my card." Shelby handed him a business card from her jacket pocket. "Call me if you think of anything that may help with the investigation."

They shook hands with the principal, then he walked them to the parking lot.

As Shelby started the engine, Erickson said, "They say don't meet your heroes, but I don't know. I was this close," he held his finger and thumb an inch apart, "to asking him for an autograph."

Shelby twisted to face him. "This is a murder investigation, Detective. I'd appreciate it if you'd take it a little more seriously."

Erickson's chin jutted forward, and he pursed his lips. He turned to mirror her position. "You want to talk serious? Why didn't you ask him more about Bobby Garza? Why didn't you get details about those 'trash talking,'" he made air quotes, "incidents? Maybe Bobby got 'worked up,'" air quotes again, "while he was with Whitney last night."

Shelby's stomach became a cauldron of boiling acid. "Bobby has to answer for himself. We can't accept hearsay as evidence."

"No," Erickson countered, "but hearsay can damn well lead us in the direction we need to go. Then we get the evidence we need to back it up." He huffed a breath, then turned away, staring out his window. "No wonder Guerrero called me in. It's like you've never been the lead on a case before." He swiveled back to her, his face set in hard lines. "This should be a slam dunk. An easy win."

Shelby's phone buzzed. She read the text. "Simon and Carter finished canvassing the neighborhood around the pool. We'll talk to them when they get back to the station." She pocketed her phone. "Hopefully, we don't hit a dead end."

"Video footage of our killer waltzing into the pool with Whitney and leaving alone?" Erickson shook his head. "That's too much to hope for." He crossed the first two fingers on both of his hands. "Let's hope forensics can tell us more about those fibers."

Five

Bobby Garza's house was only a few streets over from the Chandler's. It was a split-level, built in the '80s, and looked exactly like its neighbors. A red-and-white yard sign with the number ninety-seven stood in the grass near the curb.

Shelby rang the doorbell. Rapid footsteps thundered toward them before the inside door swung open. A tall, dark boy with a wiry build stared at them through the glass of the storm door. His wide eyes were swollen and red.

From inside, a woman's voice called, "Bobby, who is it?" Then a middle-aged woman with close cropped hair came down the steps and moved Bobby aside to open the storm door. "Can I help you?"

"Hi, Mrs. Garza? I'm Detective Reed and this is Detective Erickson."

Mrs. Garza's eyes darted between the detectives. "What's this about?" Behind her, Bobby's eyes fell to the floor.

"It's about a student at Bellmoor. May we come in?"

Bobby's mother rounded on him. "Have you been in another fight?"

Bobby opened his mouth, but Erickson said, "Not a fight. We can explain everything inside."

Mrs. Garza eyed the detectives before nodding toward the stairs. "Come on in. Wipe your feet, please." Bobby let them pass without a word.

After everyone was settled in the living room upstairs, Shelby took out her notebook and pen. "Mrs. Garza, Bobby, I'm afraid I have sad news." Mrs. Garza looked confused, while Bobby stared at his clasped hands between his knees. "Whitney Chandler was murdered last night."

"Oh, my Lord," Mrs. Garza said, pressing her hand into her chest. "That dear girl."

Shelby watched Bobby closely. He pinched his eyes with his forefinger and thumb, swallowing hard.

"I'm guessing, Bobby, that you already knew she was dead." Shelby studied him. "It looks like you've been crying."

Bobby's eyes met Shelby's as her mother stared at her son. "Bobby, did you know?"

Bobby nodded. "Mr. Chandler called me. He thought I should know."

Shelby pressed her mouth closed against a groan. If Bobby was the killer, then Jeremy Chandler had given him time to get rid of incriminating evidence and to come up with a plausible cover story. Not to mention that word would spread through Locust Grove faster than an ill wind. She thought working in a small town would be easier than Pittsburgh. Now she had doubts.

Erickson said, "You and Whitney must have been pretty close for her parents to call you like that."

Mrs. Garza said, "They're good people. Always so kind to my Bobby. And Whitney," her voice broke, "was such a wonderful girl. Excuse me." Mrs. Garza left the room.

"Bobby," Erickson continued, "where were you last night?"

Mrs. Garza returned with a box of tissues, dabbing at her eyes and nose. "Wait a minute. You don't think my son had anything to do with this, do you?"

Shelby said, "We're just establishing a timeline of the crime, Mrs. Garza. If we can pinpoint everyone's whereabouts, what they might have seen or heard, it can help us fill in the blanks."

Erickson glanced at her with raised eyebrows. She held his gaze. He turned back to Bobby. "We know you had a game last night. How about after that?"

"All the kids came here," Mrs. Garza said. "All the football moms take turns hosting the afterparty. Well, I say 'host,' but all I do is buy the food and let the kids use the house. Bobby was really the host."

"How many kids were at the afterparty?" Shelby asked, picturing a tangled mass of teens spilling drinks and tramping dirt all over the house.

Bobby shrugged. "About forty. It's mostly the players and their girl-friends." He rubbed his forehead, his eyes wet.

Mrs. Garza gasped. "Oh, my God. I just realized. Last night is the last time I'll ever see Whitney again." Her face crumpled as she covered it with a tissue.

Shelby gave her a moment, then asked, "Mrs. Garza, what did you and your husband do while the party was going on?" Her phone buzzed in her pocket, but she ignored it.

"The kids usually stay in the basement rec room, so we stay in our room. We have a TV in there. After we're done watching our shows, we just go to bed. We know Bobby will make sure everyone behaves and gets home safely." She squeezed her son's shoulder.

Erickson turned to Bobby. "So, you were here the whole time? Did you go out at all during the party? Maybe for more food or drinks?"

"No. I was here the whole time." He directed his comment to the floor, keeping his tearful eyes averted.

His mother, also with tears brimming in her eyes, rubbed her hand over his back. "He and his friend Del stay till the bitter end, cleaning up." She turned to the detectives. "That's my only rule. Bobby has to clean up the house. Well, no booze is the other rule, but I don't worry about that. They're all good kids."

Shelby not only had investigated plenty of cases where good kids turned out to have dangerous secrets, but she also remembered what it was like to be a teen. To this day, she's thankful her parents didn't know half of what she did in high school. And she graduated at the top of her class.

"Who's your friend? Del?" Erickson asked.

"Del Coleman," Mrs. Garza answered. "He's on the team, too." Shelby made a note.

"Is he? What position?"

Bobby answered, "He's on the D-line with me."

"So, a big guy like you?" Erickson gave Bobby a half-smile.

"Yeah, I guess."

"Bobby," Shelby shifted in her seat, "is there anyone who didn't like Whitney? We know she was an excellent student, but sometimes people get jealous. Can you think of anyone who had it out for Whitney?"

"No." Bobby sat up, shaking his head. "Whitney was the best. She was nice to everyone. And if anyone needed help with a class or something, she would tutor them. Seriously. I can't believe she's gone." Covering his face with his hand, Bobby broke down, finally letting out his grief.

Mrs. Garza pulled Bobby into a hug, tears sliding down her cheeks. Shelby met Erickson's eyes. The Garzas' grief was raw. She felt they'd asked enough questions for now. He nodded.

Shelby took a business card from her pocket and set it on the coffee table. "Mrs. Garza, Bobby, if either of you or your husband think of anything that will help us with the investigation, please don't hesitate to give me a call."

The detectives stood and made for the short flight of stairs that led to the front door. Mrs. Garza stayed in the living room, quietly sobbing, but Bobby followed them to the door. He opened it for them, shuffling his feet and darting his eyes around the landing. Shelby realized, standing right next to Bobby, that he was a big guy. Taller than Erickson, with large hands and feet, and broad shoulders. In a few years, with several pounds of additional muscle, he could go toe to toe with an NFL player.

She was about to say goodbye when Bobby braced his arm across the doorway. She drew back. His eyes were dark and intense. He said quietly, "Look, I know I'm a suspect. I'm her boyfriend and all the true crime stories say it's always the partner. But I want you to know: I didn't do it. I was here all night. You can ask anyone from the party. Just find out who did this to Whitney, okay?"

An icy chill ran down Shelby's spine and her mouth ran dry. She couldn't speak. She could only stare back at Bobby.

Finally, Erickson said, "We'll be in touch."

Then they were back in Shelby's car, her hands on the wheel. Erickson said, "That was an interesting speech." He tipped his head, trying to find Shelby's eyes. "Don't you think?"

"Yeah, interesting." Her fingers were like icicles resting on the steering wheel. She swallowed. "His hands are pretty big. Maybe the right size to match the pattern of bruising on Shelby's neck." Then she met Erickson's eyes. "But he said he was here all night. And he had a house full of witnesses."

"Until they went home. His parents can't vouch that he was here all night. They were tucked up in bed."

"We'll have to talk to Del Coleman. I got a text while we were talking to the Garzas." She pulled out her phone. "Forensics has more info for us."

Erickson buckled his seatbelt. "Good. Let's head back to the station. I could use a snack."

Six

"**M**m, that's tasty." Erickson dabbed at his mouth with a napkin. "I think this is the best pepperoni roll I've ever had. And from a gas station. Who'da thunk it?" Erickson grinned.

"Gas stations around here can surprise you. People rely on them. Too many food deserts." Shelby took a sip of her sweet tea.

Instead of making a lunch of donuts and pastries, Shelby had insisted they stop on the way back to the station for real food. The local Sunoco stocked fresh takeout, including his pepperoni rolls and her chicken tenders and side salad.

When they returned to the police station, several other officers were eating their lunches at their desks, including Naomi. She had a stack of oversized books next to her Cup O'Noodle.

Erickson had tapped the stack with a knuckle. "Whatcha got there, Office Kim?"

She gave him a bashful glance, then turned to Shelby. "I'm going through yearbooks from Bellmoor Prep, looking at candid photos to see if we can connect Whitney with someone we haven't heard about yet."

Shelby lifted her eyebrows and felt herself smile. Seeing Naomi take the initiative made her proud. "Well done. Anything so far?"

Naomi shook her head. "Not so far. A few pictures of her with Bobby at games and dances. Two with her and Skye."

After a sip of his grape soda, Erickson said, "Skye? That's the BFF, right?"

"Alleged BFF," Naomi replied. "Possibly more like frenemy."

"The plot thickens." He winked at the young officer, and she dropped her eyes.

Shelby eyed Erickson, saying to Naomi, "We'll be in the conference room."

Now they were seated at the long table, a nearly empty whiteboard taunting them. Shelby's eyes traced the crime scene photos, school photos of Whitney, Bobby, and Skye, and a professional headshot of Principal Wheeler. Shelby had written a handful of bullet points under each photo, drawing a few red lines in between. They had precious little evidence so far. With a tiny ember of hope burning in her breast, she dialed the number for forensics and put them on speakerphone.

"Forensics," a male voice answered. Probably the same officer from the crime scene. Shelby didn't know his name. She should.

"It's Detective Reed."

"And Erickson." Erickson winked at her.

She ignored him. "I got your text. What do you have?"

"Cause of death was definitely strangulation. Big hands, very strong, according to the contusions. Whoever it was crushed her windpipe. Being dropped into the deep end also broke some bones. Best we can tell the killer strangled her up above, then rolled her into the pool."

"Why bother rolling her into the pool?" Erickson bit into another pepperoni roll. "Why not hotfoot it out of there?"

"Probably to delay discovery as long as possible," Shelby replied. "If Whitney lay there until May, when they opened the pool for the summer, trace evidence would be gone."

"Most likely," said the voice on the phone. "As for those fibers, they were mostly nylon, with a small amount of Spandex."

"Spandex?" Shelby said. "I was thinking they came from a windbreaker. Are windbreakers made of Spandex?"

"No, but football jerseys are."

Shelby reluctantly met Erickson's eyes across the table. Although he said nothing, his expression said "I told you so."

She closed her eyes. "If we bring you a jersey, and you run a comparison, is a solid match possible, or is it iffy?"

"Not to a specific jersey, but the type of jersey, yes."

Erickson frowned. "No DNA on the fibers?"

"None that we could extract."

Erickson nodded.

Shelby stared out the window at the autumn colors clinging to the tree branches. "Anything else?"

"No sexual assault. No injuries other than the ones caused by the strangulation and the drop. No fingerprints or foreign DNA. The killer kept it simple and clean."

"What about the girl's bedroom?"

"Didn't find anything unusual. Although, she had a pretty sweet setup for making TikToks."

Shelby ran her tongue around her teeth. "All right. Thanks for the update." She ended the call and took a bite of salad. She refused to look at Erickson's smug face. "Technically, it could have been anyone wearing a Bobcats jersey."

He slumped in his chair and took another bite of his pepperoni roll. "Technically, yes. But we have someone who owns and wears a football jersey," he raised one finger, "has the hands of a giant," raised a second finger, "and is known to get violent." He raised a third finger and narrowed his eyes.

Shelby could feel Erickson's aggravation prickling against her skin.

She said, "This kill was 'simple and clean,' according to forensics. Do you think a hotheaded teenage boy would be 'simple and clean?' No. If Bobby killed Whitney, it would have been in the heat of the moment. It wouldn't have been premeditated because, according to everyone we've spoken to so far, they weren't fighting, and they were happy." She scrubbed her hands with a paper napkin. "There were no prints at the scene. You think he brought gloves? The teenage boys I know can hardly remember to take their wallets and keys with them when they leave the house, let alone a pair of gloves."

Erickson sat up so abruptly he almost launched his chair into the wall of filing cabinets behind him. "Why are you dodging this? Why don't you want it to be Bobby?"

Shelby gathered her trash and stood, pushing her own chair back. "It's not that I don't want it to be Bobby. I don't know that kid from Adam. I just want to make sure we're looking at all the angles. That we're not wearing blinders because it's an easy answer."

He stood, tossed his trash, and followed her into the bullpen. "Just because the answer is easy doesn't make it wrong." He lengthened his stride to catch her up as she reached her desk. "Hey." She stopped and glared at him. He glanced at the other officers, then chucked his head toward the hallway that led to the restrooms. She followed him. His gaze was earnest and intense. "I don't know what's going on with you, but I'd love to. Fill me in. There's clearly something happening with you I know nothing about. Maybe I can help." He rested his hands on his hips. "No, I know I can help. As partners, we should have each other's backs. And I can't do that without all the facts."

Shelby searched his eyes. His cavalier attitude was gone. He was serious and genuinely interested in what was wrong with her. But she never discussed what had happened with anyone at the station. It was personal. It was private. And if she started talking about it, she didn't know if she'd still be standing after she finished.

It had been so long since someone had tried to reach her, inside, where she was hiding in the dark. A tremor ran through her at the thought of letting go, loosening her grip on feelings that threatened to consume her if she didn't keep them squeezed in tight. Erickson waited.

She swallowed. "You're right. My past is clouding my judgement. I'll do better."

He waited another beat, then dropped his gaze to the floor. The fluorescent light bounced off his golden hair. He shook his head, then met her gaze, his brown eyes flinty. "We need to solve this case. I need to solve this case." His voice held a pleading note she didn't understand. Then his expression softened. "When you're ready. I'm here. This job?" He looked back at the bullpen, then at her. "This job can blacken your soul if you let it."

Shelby's breath caught in her chest and the back of her neck tingled. For the first time in ages, a tiny light glowed in that darkness inside her. Sunshiny Erickson wasn't the two-dimensional cartoon character she'd thought he was. She only had a moment to wonder in what way this job had darkened his soul before they were interrupted.

"Reed. Erickson." Captain Guerrero stepped into the hallway. "Come to my office and update me on where we are so far." She walked away, heels clicking on the linoleum.

Erickson shrugged. "Discussion of your existential crisis is tabled for another time." He gestured toward the door for Shelby to lead the way.

She took a deep breath and followed her boss.

Seven

Whereas the rest of the station smelled like stale coffee, mold, and a hint of wet dog, the captain's office smelled of lemon polish and her perfume, something sweet and floral. Her desk was shabby, like the rest of the desks in the bullpen, but it was neat, everything in its place. Shelby and Erickson sat in the scarred, but gleaming, armchairs in front of her desk.

Captain Guerrero rested her clasped hands on an open file. Her bored expression belied the sharp mind and gravitas that made Guerrero an effective leader. "Where are we?"

Erickson crossed an ankle over his knee and looked at Shelby. Apparently, she was taking the lead. "Unfortunately, we don't know much more than we did this morning."

Guerrero pressed her lips together, then said, "Fill me in."

Shelby pulled out her notebook. "Whitney was last seen around six p.m. by her parents. At that point, Whitney's friend Skye Stevens picked her up to go to the football game. At approximately nine-thirty p.m., Mrs. Chandler received a text from Whitney saying that she was going to an after-party at Bobby Garza's house."

Erickson tapped his knee with his hand. "He's her boyfriend."

Shelby glanced up. "Yes." She went back to her notes. "We spoke to Bobby and his mother. His father wasn't home. They didn't tell us anything we didn't know after speaking with the Chandlers. She went to the game, then the after-party at Bobby's."

"Who did she leave with?"

Erickson glanced at Shelby. "No one. Skye, the friend who gave her a ride to the game, left the party early without Whitney."

"We also spoke to Principal Alfred Wheeler," Shelby said. "He says Whitney was a model student. In fact," she looked up from her notebook, "everyone we've spoken to says no one disliked Whitney. She was popular, well-liked. No one had a beef with her. She wasn't fighting with anyone. No one could think of anyone who dislikes her."

Guerrero raised an eyebrow. "A teenage girl who isn't fighting with someone? That's difficult to believe. Teenage girls are nothing but drama. At least, in my experience." Shelby knew Guerrero had a daughter who went to the public high school. No doubt she spoke from personal experience.

"Although," Erickson shifted in his seat. "Her boyfriend, Bobby, has a history of fighting."

"With other boys, rival football players." Shelby shot Erickson a sharp look. She returned her attention to Guerrero. "The principal, and her parents, and Bobby's parents, said the two of them never fought. That he adored her."

"Does he have an alibi?" Guerrero asked.

Erickson said, "His parents say he was home all night."

"But you don't believe them?"

His eyes narrowed as he considered her question. "I don't think they're covering for him. But we've all been teens. We know what they get up to. He could have snuck out during the night."

Shelby addressed Guerrero. "But why would he? Whitney had been at his house for the party. Why set up a later meeting time in a deserted, cold area? If they wanted to fool around, they could have just waited for the other kids to leave. If they were fighting—and no one thinks they were—why not just have it out at the house?"

Guerrero, eyebrows raised in question, looked at Erickson. He shrugged. She said to Shelby, "Forensics?"

Shelby replied, "Nothing we can use so far. They pulled clothing fibers from the body. No DNA."

"Anything on her phone? Recent calls, texts?"

Shelby shook her head. "Her phone and her purse are missing. Her locker's being searched." She made a note in her notebook. "We'll get a warrant to pull phone records. Maybe an erroneous number will show up."

"Or a juicy voicemail," Erickson added.

Guerrero sighed and rolled her lips. "What's next?"

Erickson dropped his foot to the floor, sitting up. "I say we pick up Bobby. Apply some pressure."

Guerrero's forehead creased. "Based on?"

Erickson looked at Guerrero, then Shelby, like they'd sprouted second heads. "History of violence. Closest to her. He wears a red football jersey." When the women didn't agree, he continued, tapping the captain's desk with his forefinger to make a point. "Data shows time and again that when someone is murdered, it's usually the partner. He's the obvious place to start."

Guerrero met Shelby's eyes. Shelby's heart rate picked up. She knew the captain's train of thought was the same as her own. But the captain was lucky enough not to have the detailed memories Shelby did. Guerrero leaned back in her chair. "The national news hasn't picked up this story yet, but it's only a matter of time." At Erickson's confused expression, she said, "A pretty white girl is murdered in a small town in West Virginia. And it involves a football player." She sighed again, meeting Shelby's eyes. "They'll want to connect dots, even if they don't exist."

Shelby nodded. Erickson glanced between them, waiting for an explanation that didn't come. For the first time, she wondered how he could be so obtuse. How did he not know what had happened? She didn't want to fill him in. He could Google it.

Guerrero stood and walked to her door. "Keep casting the net. Talk to Skye Stevens, Whitney's other friends, Bobby's friends, and her teachers. Paint a clearer picture, fill in the timeline."

Shelby and Erickson stood to leave. Erickson placed his hands on his hips. "And Bobby Garza?"

Guerrero lifted her chin. "I'm glad I called you in, Detective Erickson. We need your objectivity." She opened her door. "Keep him in mind, but also keep an open mind."

They left the captain's office. Shelby knew Erickson was confused and probably deserved more information, but she wasn't feeling charitable.

"Detectives," Officer Simon called to them from the bullpen.

When they joined him, Erickson said, "What's up, Will?"

"Carter and I talked to everyone who lives around the pool." He glanced at Shelby, but spoke to Erickson, standing close. He reminded Shelby of a puppy hoping for a pat on the head.

"And?"

"No cameras. At least, none pointing toward the pool. Only two houses had security cameras, and they're focused on their backyards."

"It was worth a shot," Shelby said.

"Good work." Erickson nodded at Will.

Shelby asked, "And the locker?"

"That's next. I wanted to come back and report on the cameras first."

"Thank you, Officer Simon."

Will grinned from ear to ear, then realized he'd been dismissed. He returned to the bullpen, a bit of swagger in his step.

Shelby walked over to Naomi's desk, where she was yawning, still poring through old yearbooks.

"Anything?"

Naomi shook her head. "Not really. So far, all the photos show exactly what we already know about Whitney. Model student, popular."

Shelby nodded, then said, "I need you to file for a warrant to request Whitney's phone records."

Naomi stifled a yawn. "On it."

"Then head home. It's been a long day."

Naomi nodded, turning to her computer.

Erickson looked at Shelby, raising his eyebrows. "Well?"

They were spinning their wheels. She knew what he was asking. They needed new information. And there was one obvious path. She nodded. "Let's go get Bobby."

A navy-blue sky greeted them when they left the station. The sun had set while they'd been inside. Shelby zipped her jacket against the chilly air, the scent of a wood fire on the breeze.

When Mrs. Garza answered the door, she informed them Bobby wasn't home.

They shared a look. Either Bobby was out with his friends, sharing his grief over Whitney's death, or he was running.

"Mrs. Garza," Erickson said, "do you know where he went? We need to speak with him."

Mrs. Garza's eyes widened. "Is he under arrest?"

Shelby's stomach felt hollow. Her scalp prickled with dread. "Not yet. But I advise you to retain a lawyer for him."

Mrs. Garza lifted her chin and straightened to her fullest height. "My boy did not kill poor Whitney. You're barking up the wrong tree."

"That could very well be. But we have questions for Bobby, and his answers could point us in the right direction." Shelby tilted her head. "Can you tell us where he went?"

Mrs. Garza's eyes darted between the detectives. She took a deep breath, wringing her hands. "I don't know."

Erickson said, "Does he share his location with you? Do you have him on Life 360 or Find My Phone?"

Mrs. Garza's chin remained stubbornly fixed. "Of course not. I trust my boy."

The detectives climbed back into Shelby's car. She started it, saying, "I'm not ready to put out an APB on Bobby. He's probably just at a friend's house, crying into a glass of Mountain Dew."

Erickson stared at her. Shelby braced for an argument. But he slumped in his seat, running a hand over his face. "I agree. We don't want to scare him, send him into hiding. Let's call it a night."

Shelby was thankful Erickson didn't put up a fight. She drove them back to the station where his car was parked. As he opened the passenger door, she spoke without overthinking her words, offering an olive branch. "Why don't I pick you up in the morning? Save you the drive and you don't have to leave your car here all day."

He gave her a playful grin. "Detective Reed, are you turning sweet on me?"

She sucked her teeth, immediately regretting her impulsive decision. "Do you want a ride or not?"

"You bet I do. Curb to curb service? That's hard to find in small towns." He winked. "I'm not passing that up." He closed the door, whistling as he walked to his car. Shelby drove away, shaking her head.

Eight

The road Erickson lived on wound between hills and hollows, under red-leafed maples and yellow ginseng trees. Shelby came around a sharp bend and would have missed his mailbox if it weren't wrapped in a magnetic Pitt Panthers cover. His address was marked in county-issued reflective numbers on the post. Black and orange "private drive" signs were stapled to trees on either side of his gravel-packed driveway. Erickson clearly wanted to avoid rubber-neckers looking for a good spot to hunt. Or to have a quickie in their car.

The driveway broke through the trees and ended in an oval gravel patch where Erickson's truck was parked, with a detached garage next to the house. His truck sported Steelers gear, including a license plate border. The house was a plain two-story box, painted white with black trim, and two wooden rocking chairs sat on the front porch. It was clean and well-kept.

Shelby knocked on the front door. Erickson called out, "Come in." She opened the door and stepped into the front hall, which split the house in two. The living room to the left looked like a photo spread straight out of *Country Living*. Colonial blue mixed with cheerful gingham and punched tin lanterns. To the right, the dining room was filled with dark wood antique furniture, including a sideboard where beeswax candles sat next to a ceramic pitcher and matching basin.

An arrangement of fake daisies and sunflowers nestled in a speckled crock.

Jasper's house was not what Shelby was expecting. There were no La-Z-Boy recliners, no video game consoles. Not even a flat screen TV. Instead, it was cozy. Shelby wondered if everyone at the station had failed to mention that Erickson had a wife.

From another room, Jasper called, "Come on back."

She walked down the dark hallway, admiring the family photos hung on the wall. Even as a boy, Jasper was handsome, missing teeth and mussed hair and all.

The hallway ended in a large, sunny kitchen that held a faint scent of cinnamon. White-washed cabinets hung from the walls. Flecked linoleum counters held more crockery and tin items. Sunlight poured in from a window over a farmhouse sink and from a large bay window that hung above a wooden booth and table. Although the kitchen was old-fashioned, the appliances were modern and top-of-the-line.

Jasper was nowhere to be found. Instead, she found a pile of boxes in the middle of the sizable vinyl floor. "Hello?"

The back door to her right opened and Jasper strode in. The door's frilly valance waved as he shoved it closed. "Hey, thanks for picking me up." He was out of breath.

She gestured at the boxes. "Moving out?"

He gave a mirthless chuckle. "Not me. My girlfriend, Imogen."

"Oh." She gave him a tight smile. "Sorry to hear that."

He waved a hand before resting his fists on his hips. "No worries. It's a tale as old as time. Boy meets girl. Boy falls in love with girl. Girl moves in. Girl has an epiphany one night at the Outlaw Music Festival that she's squandering her life in a small town with her small-town boyfriend and moves to Seattle."

Shelby's eyes popped. "Wow."

"Yeah." Jasper mimicked his head exploding with his hands. "Wow."

"Why Seattle?"

He rolled his eyes. "She met a girl at Outlaw who went to school at the University of Washington. She went on and on about the 'culture' in Seattle," he gave the word air quotes. "Now she's convinced she should be a singer or sculptor or goddam ventriloquist or something."

Shelby bit her lip to keep from grinning. She shoved her hands into her jeans pockets. "And she can't do that in Locust Grove?"

He shrugged. "Apparently not. Not a big enough audience." He rolled his eyes again, then frowned. "To be honest, it's for the best. We'd been fighting about my hours, how much I work. She didn't like being alone so much."

Shelby nodded. That was one thing she'd loved about her late husband. He'd understood what was required of her at work. He hadn't been needy. But when they were together, he'd been as romantic as she could have wished for.

"She even suggested I go into private security so I could have regular hours," Erickson said, shoving a box aside with his foot.

Shelby grimaced. Suggesting becoming a mall cop to a police detective was like suggesting a chef trained at Le Cordon Bleu become a line cook at Eat 'N' Park. "For the best, then."

He nodded, then gestured to the boxes. "I was just carrying these to the back patio. Her brother is coming by to pick them up sometime today."

Shelby dropped her keys on the kitchen table. "Want some help?"

His face lit up. "Yeah. Thanks."

They made quick work, moving the boxes to the stone patio. Shelby admired the pots of burgundy mums that dotted the perimeter. She had planted nothing this year. The only show of color in her yard so far had been the volunteer petunias that had sprouted in her front flower bed.

Jasper dropped the last box on the pile, and they returned to the kitchen. "Cup of coffee before we go?"

She glanced at her watch.

He laughed. "Don't worry, Boss. We'll make it quick." She sat in the booth as he moved toward an impressive-looking coffee machine and chose a pod from a rotating rack. He took a mug from a cabinet and popped the pod into the machine. It whirred to life. "I haven't met my caffeine quota for the morning yet. And you have to try this hazelnut blend I found at Kroger. It's mighty tasty." He looked at her over his shoulder. "I mean, Kroger. Who knew?"

He fixed her coffee to her liking, after asking first, then made his own. He brought both mugs to the table and sat on the opposite side of the booth. She sipped and hummed appreciatively.

"I know, right?" Jasper sipped his own coffee, closed his eyes, smacked his lips and let out a dramatic sigh. "Kroger."

She huffed a quick laugh, hiding it behind her mug. "I have to say, Erickson, that your house wasn't what I was expecting." She glanced out the bay window where a bird feeder hung. While she watched, a dazzling goldfinch lit onto a perch, tilting its head before pecking at the seeds inside.

"Let me guess." He rested his forearms on the table. "You thought you'd walk into something between a sports bar and the Playboy mansion?"

She wrinkled her nose. "Something like that." Her eyes roamed the homey kitchen. "This is so... domestic."

He barked a deep laugh. "It should be. My mom was the best home-maker ever."

Her eyebrows lifted. "Was?"

"Oh," he raised a hand in a stop gesture. "She's not dead. She and my dad moved to Florida about two years ago, after he retired. They couldn't take the winters anymore."

"So, they gave you the house?" She raised her mug. "Nice."

"No kidding." He leaned forward. "Between the cost of real estate and my student loan debt, I'd never be able to afford a house and property like this."

Shelby nodded, familiar with that struggle. She and Shawn had practically dug change out of the couch cushions and nearby gutters to afford a home. And that was on two incomes.

"They have a condo in Fort Lauderdale," Erickson continued. "It's awesome. I go there for holidays and my yearly vacation now."

"How could they afford it if they didn't sell this house?" As high as the real estate prices were in Locust Grove, West Virginia, the prices in Fort Lauderdale had to be astronomical. Then she recalled herself, dropping her eyes to her coffee. Heat tickled her cheeks. "Sorry. That was out of line."

He tapped the table, bringing her attention back to him. His brown eyes warmed and his smile was soft. "I'm an open book, Detective. No worries." He sat up and looked out the window. Now a robin dined at the feeder, dropping bits from its beak. "This farm has been in my dad's family for three generations. It was a successful hay farm until my dad's time. Then costs started outweighing the profits, and the land became more valuable than anything we could grow. So, he and mom sold off the surrounding acres to a developer. That's what they used to move to Fort Lauderdale. They're set up real nice."

Shelby frowned. "What about siblings? No one else wanted to stake a claim on this beautiful home?"

He winked at her, and she barely suppressed an eye roll. "Always detecting." He set down his empty mug. "No siblings. I'm an only child. Mom and Dad had me kind of late. I was their last shot at having kids." He raised his mug. "The reigning prince."

Shelby tipped her mug to him, playing along. She looked out the window again. "You're lucky. Your parents sound wonderful, and you don't have to deal with—" She stopped. His dratted cheery disposition was knocking down her guard. She pressed her lips together.

He squinted at her. "Don't have to deal with what?"

She sipped her coffee, then said, "Nosy neighbors. It's so beautiful here. I hate to think your view will be the backs of other houses."

He shook his finger. "Oh, no. Mom and Dad knew what they were doing. They kept enough acreage around the house to make it still seem secluded. And the way the hills lie," he curved his hand up and down through the air, "I'll have plenty of privacy. Although," he clasped his hands behind his head, displaying his broad chest and hefty shoulders. "I would have been happy to provide a show for any ladies lucky enough to buy a house in my backyard."

Now Shelby rolled her eyes. "On that note, we need to get going."

"Yes, we do." He swept up their mugs and placed them in the sink. He grabbed a jacket off a hall tree by the front door as they left. "And our agenda today?"

"We're starting at Del's. I called Mrs. Garza on the way here. She said Bobby didn't come home last night." She glanced at Erickson. His jaw hardened. "She assumed Bobby spent the night, so we're headed to Del's."

"That's Del Coleman?" Erickson asked.

"Yes."

"Did Bobby drive? Walk?"

"He walked. His house isn't far from Del's." They got in Shelby's car. She faced Erickson, a hard ball of tension in the pit of her stomach. "My gut tells me we won't find him at Del's."

Erickson buckled his seatbelt. "My gut agrees with yours." He slapped the dashboard. "Silver lining? If we don't find Bobby, we can still talk to Del. Check that off our list."

"True." She maneuvered onto the main road and headed toward Del's. "But in my experience, a silver lining just means you're in the eye of the storm, and you'd better hang on for dear life."

Nine

Del Coleman was as tall and broad-shouldered as Bobby Garza, but where Bobby was cut with muscle, Del was pudgier. Golden curls topped his head, and his face was pale with rough, reddened cheeks.

He and his father sat in armchairs in the Coleman's living room. Hummel figurines stared at Shelby and Erickson, who sat on the couch, from every horizontal surface.

Bobby was nowhere to be seen.

Del had his hands clasped in front of his mouth, elbows on knees, glancing between the detectives.

Mr. Coleman said, "Can I get you anything?"

"No, thank you." Shelby addressed Del. "When was the last time you saw Bobby?"

"Dear God," Mr. Coleman whispered. "Did something happen to Bobby, too?"

Shelby said, "We just need to ask him some questions, and his mother said we could find him here. Del?"

Del's right knee bounced hard enough to jostle his hands. "He's not here. Last time I saw him was at his house, at the after-party."

"What time did you leave?" Erickson asked.

Del glanced at his father. "About midnight, when the party broke up."

"That's true," Mr. Coleman said. "I heard Del come in about twenty after twelve. I stayed awake until I knew he was home."

"Did you see him come in?"

"No. He has a key, so he let himself in. Then I went to sleep."

"Was your wife already asleep?"

"She wasn't here. She works nights at the hospital. She's a nurse." Mr. Coleman gave Del a tight smile and gripped his shoulder briefly. Del's knee continued to bounce.

Shelby said, "Have you heard from Bobby today?"

Del nodded, chewing his upper lip. "He texted me. Said he'd see me later." He pressed his lips together and swallowed hard.

"Did he say when?"

Del shook his head.

"Were you friends with Whitney?"

Del nodded again. "Yeah. Me, Bobby, and Whitney are all tight." His eyes grew shiny. "I can't believe she's dead."

Mr. Coleman shook his head. "Who would want to kill that sweet girl? She had such a bright future ahead of her."

Del's knee stopped bouncing. He rubbed the center of his forehead, hiding his wet eyes.

Shelby's phone buzzed. She quickly checked her screen. It was a text from her father.

Dad: Don't forget about tonight.

Erickson glanced at her with raised eyebrows. She gave her head a tiny shake and set her phone aside.

"Del," Erickson said, "did Bobby and Whitney ever fight? Any drama between them?"

Del shook his head. "No. They got along great."

"Bobby gets rough on the field, but he treated Whitney very well," Mr. Coleman said.

Erickson gave him a small smile. "That's what we've heard." He turned back to Del. "Was Bobby wearing his jersey Friday night? After the game?"

Del frowned. "Not his game jersey. It was sweaty and gross. But he was wearing his school jersey."

"School jersey?" Shelby made a note while Erickson gave the Colemans a confused look.

Mr. Coleman said, "All the boys on the team have a jersey they keep clean so they can wear it to school on game day. Then they wear them after the game. Kind of a tradition."

"So," Shelby said, "all the team members wore their school jerseys after the game on Friday night? At the party?"

Del nodded.

Shelby's eyes met Erickson's. No doubt he was thinking the same thing she was, that their investigation just got more complicated.

Shelby said, "Del, can you think of anyone who didn't like Whitney? Maybe she was fighting with someone? Got on someone's bad side?"

Del stared at Shelby for a moment before saying, "The only person who doesn't like Whitney sometimes is Skye, but they're kinda friends. And, I mean, Skye wouldn't kill anyone. She's nice."

Erickson said, "Do you know where Bobby could be? Does he have a favorite hangout? A secret treehouse?" Erickson flashed a mischievous smile.

Del shrugged his beefy shoulders, his eyes on the ground. "I don't know. He usually sleeps in when we don't have school. Sometimes we play video games, but we go to his house or mine." He started chewing his upper lip again.

Mr. Coleman's phone rang. He checked the screen and said, "I have to take this. Are we finished?"

Shelby nodded. "For now. Thank you for your time."

Mr. Coleman disappeared down the hallway while Shelby and Erickson stood, heading toward the front door.

When they stepped outside, Del followed them. He shifted his weight between his feet while Shelby and Erickson waited. He clearly had something to say that he didn't want his father to hear.

"What is it, Del?" Shelby asked.

He looked pained, hands shoved into the pockets of his joggers. "I don't know if I should say or not."

Shelby looked at Erickson, who tipped his head toward Del. "Del," she said, "you want us to catch Whitney's killer, right?"

He blanched. "Of course, I do. But I don't want to say anything that would get someone in trouble if it doesn't mean anything."

"We understand," Erickson said. "But it's our job to figure out what's related to the case and what's not. And we won't tell anyone you were the person who shared whatever it is you want to tell us."

Del nodded. He took a breath big enough to inflate his barrel chest, then let it out through puffed cheeks. "Okay." He gripped the back of his neck. "Drugs."

That was all he said. Shelby and Erickson exchanged silent glances, hoping for more. They had been expecting Del to say something about Bobby.

Shelby asked, "What do you mean 'drugs?'"

Del winced. "Look, sometimes Whitney took drugs."

"Like what?" Shelby took out her notebook and pen.

Del glanced at her notebook, then said, "If she had a big test or term papers or something, she'd take Adderall to help her focus. But then she'd take Valium to help her sleep if she was wired, you know?" Del was chewing his lip so hard it was in danger of breaking and bleeding.

"Where did she get the pills?" Erickson asked.

Del shrugged. "I don't know. She didn't do it a lot. Just, like, when she really needed to." He looked between the detectives. "I know it bothered Bobby."

Erickson squinted. "Bothered him enough to make him angry?"

Del reared back. "No. No way, man. He said something to her about how he didn't like it, but he wasn't angry." He looked at his feet. "It wasn't like that."

Shelby pursed her lips. "Del, did it bother you? Did you ever have feelings for Whitney?"

"What? No!" A blotchy shade of crimson crept up the boy's face. "She was just a friend." His eyes welled up. "One of my best friends." He looked away, across the street where a kid was shooting a basketball. "I don't know what we're going to do now."

"About what?"

Del's attention snapped back to Shelby. "Nothing. I didn't mean anything. Just," he searched for words, "I just meant she helped us with our homework and studying and stuff. Now she's gone." He wiped his eyes.

"Del?" Mr. Coleman called from inside the house.

Del looked like he'd been zapped with a cattle prod. Shelby thought he was awfully nervous. "I have to go." He stuffed his giant hand into the mailbox hanging by the front door, pulled out a stack of mail, then disappeared back into the house.

Shelby and Erickson sat in her car; each one lost in their thoughts.

After a minute, Shelby said, "He didn't give us the whole story."

Erickson pursed his lips. "Nope."

"Whitney can't be the only student using."

"Nope." Erickson rested his elbow on the passenger door and rubbed his temple. "And someone sold her those drugs."

Shelby caught Erickson's gaze. "We need to search her room ourselves. We're missing something. And we need to talk to Bobby again."

Ten

Before Shelby and Erickson knocked on the Chandler's front door, Shelby had called the station to put out a be-on-the-lookout on Bobby Garza. He wasn't driving, so he couldn't have gone far. He might have hitchhiked, but Shelby doubted it. Kids today weren't that stupid.

Mrs. Chandler, with a pale face and shadows under her eyes, opened the door. "Is it over? Did you find Whitney's killer?" Her eyes shined with hope.

"I'm sorry, Mrs. Chandler. Not yet." Shelby offered her a rueful smile. "However, we'd like to search Whitney's room."

Her forehead wrinkled. "I thought the police already did that." Mrs. Chandler looked over her shoulder. She hesitated.

"Yes, our forensics team searched her room. But sometimes, as detectives, we know what to look for, once we've gathered more information."

"We can get a warrant if we need to," Erickson said in a kind voice. "But it will save us a lot of precious time if we can check it over with your permission."

Mrs. Chandler's mouth twisted. "I haven't been in there yet. There might be dirty clothes on the floor or..." Her voice trailed away, her throat working.

Shelby nodded. "We understand you don't want to invade your daughter's privacy. But we might find something that will help us with the investigation. You want that for Whitney, right?"

"Of course." Mrs. Chandler straightened and pressed her lips together. "Of course, Detectives. Please, come in." She stood aside to let them enter.

Whitney's room was exactly what Shelby expected it to be. A soft white comforter covered her bed, Squishmallows sat between blush pink pillows, and a makeshift video studio took up a corner of the room. Jewelry and mementos covered the top of her dresser. Makeup and hair accessories lay scattered across the vanity. Polaroids were tucked all around the vanity mirror. Shelby examined these first as she snapped on her nitrile gloves.

She touched a picture of Whitney holding a bouquet and standing next to Bobby, who wore a sharp suit. They stood in front of a fall background, probably last year's homecoming dance. There was also a picture of Whitney in the same dress dancing with Del, both of them smiling. Two other pictures showed Whitney and a girl she assumed was Skye, holding awards, with a teacher standing behind them, a wide smile on his face. There were more pictures of Whitney with Bobby or Del or both of them.

One picture caught Shelby's eye. She pulled it from the mirror's frame. Three rows of teens crammed onto and in front of a couch in what looked like a basement rec room. All the boys were wearing red jerseys.

"Hey." Shelby waved it at Erickson. He stopped sifting through the mementos on the dresser and took the photo from Shelby in his gloved hand. "Think this is an after-game party?"

"Yeah, at Bobby's house." He squinted at the picture. "There's Del and Whitney. I don't see Bobby."

"Maybe he's taking the picture."

"Could be."

Shelby nodded. "I think that's Skye." She pointed to a pretty girl with long brown hair.

"Keeper?" Erickson lifted his eyebrows. Shelby nodded, and he placed it in an evidence bag. She also snapped photos with her phone of the other Polaroids around the mirror.

They continued to comb through Whitney's room, Whitney's life. A worn, faded stuffed bunny lay under her comforter. Old birthday cards fell out of her collection of *The Lunar Chronicles* and *The Baby-Sitters Club* books. A box of condoms sat at the back of her underwear drawer, rolled in a pair of black lace panties. They bagged it for prints. Forensics had already taken her laptop and school iPad.

Del told them Whitney took Adderall and Valium, but they didn't find any drugs in her room. Erickson slipped out and checked the medicine cabinet in the bathroom, but came up with nothing. They stood in the center of her room, hands on hips, heads swiveling while they tried to understand the mind of a teenaged girl. Where would she hide something? They lifted her mattress and box spring. They felt the bottoms of the dresser drawers. Same with her vanity. They dug into her pillowcases and empty purses. They searched the pockets of all her clothing. They shook out her shoes. Nothing.

Shelby sat on Whitney's bed, stress drawing her muscles tight as a tripwire. They'd been working the case for only a short time and already she could feel their murderer slipping away, clues falling through the cracks like sand. Their obvious suspect was on the run. They'd only scratched the surface of the secrets these kids were probably hiding. And their search of Whitney's room, which should have been a slam dunk, was fruitless.

She thought about the young girl at the bottom of the empty pool. Her mottled skin had once been like porcelain. Muck from the autumn puddles had stained her once-blonde hair. Her blue eyes were vacant and lifeless. She'd been a bright, beautiful girl. The kind who posted TikTok dances and cute selfies using her DIY studio. Eyeing Whitney's smartphone tripod, backdrop, and two tall LED lamps,

Shelby said, "Let's have Naomi put Whitney's social media under a microscope. Watch and listen to every damn TikTok or whatever for anything unusual, any clues."

Erickson followed her gaze to the equipment. He walked toward the tripod. "Thank God social media didn't exist when I was a kid. Every stupid thing I ever did would live forever." He stepped in front of it. "Like that time at a bonfire I thought I could chug a two-liter of Sprite to impress Tiffany Brown and ended up barfing all over myself." He glanced around the corner. "These lamps are cool. I wonder what kinds of videos she made." He turned on one, but the other didn't work. "Must be dead. I wonder if it charges with a USB cord." He picked up the lamp, but it slipped out of his hands. "Oh, shit." The lamp bounced on the carpet, the rectangular shade popping off. He stared at the floor. "Double shit."

Shelby stood from the bed. "Would you look at that?"

His face split into a proud grin. Small plastic packets and an old flip phone littered the floor. As he set the now empty lamp to the side, he said, "Our enterprising girl was one smart cookie."

"Too smart for her own good, though, since she's dead." Shelby kneeled on the floor and examined the packets and the phone.

"Thanks for the reminder." Erickson joined her on the floor, opening the flip phone. "All charged up. There's a handful of the same numbers in here. No names." He pressed a few buttons. "Lots of texts, but nothing of note. Abbreviations, most likely for drug names. Then dates and times."

Shelby nodded, holding a packet of white tablets. "Whitney wasn't just using. She was dealing."

Erickson met her eyes. "Looks like. Think Del knew when he told us?"

Shelby shrugged. "I don't think so, but we'll have to follow up."

Erickson focused on the list of phone numbers again. "One number shows up more than the others, no drug names. Maybe that's her supplier."

Shelby spread the plastic packets across Whitney's white comforter. "Looks like we've got Adderall, OxyContin, Xanax, Ritalin."

Erickson pointed his finger. "And Valium."

Shelby's eyes darted around the room. "Why would Whitney sell drugs? Why did she need the money? Does it look like she was living a Kardashian lifestyle?"

Erickson shook his head. "Nope. She didn't even have her own car." He pursed his lips. "Let's talk to the Chandlers."

Shelby's gut twisted at the thought of shattering the Chandlers' wholesome image of their little girl, but they needed answers.

They found Whitney's parents in the kitchen, sitting at the table, mugs in their hands, tears in their eyes.

Mr. Chandler sniffed and said, "Get what you needed?"

Shelby nodded. "We think so." She laid the plastic evidence bag holding Whitney's drug cache on the table.

"What's that?" Mrs. Chandler asked.

"Mr. and Mrs. Chandler, there's no easy way to say this, but we think Whitney was selling prescription drugs to other students."

The color drained from Mrs. Chandler's face, while Mr. Chandler stood from his chair. "How dare you? Not our Whitney. She was a good girl." He swiped his hand toward the bag of pill packets, as if to grab it, but Shelby was too quick. Mr. Chandler stared at the bag in Shelby's hand as if she held a snake.

Erickson stepped forward. "It's not uncommon for kids to keep secrets from their parents, especially something of this magnitude. We're not surprised you didn't know."

"You don't understand," Mr. Chandler said through gritted teeth. "That's not Whitney. She wouldn't do that." He pointed at the pills. "Those can't be hers. She must have been keeping them for someone."

"Mr. Chandler," Shelby said, "I've been a cop for quite a while. So has Detective Erickson. We know a dealer's stash when we see one. We found a lot of pills and a burner phone in her room."

Mrs. Chandler sobbed and covered her mouth.

"No," Mr. Chandler said. "I refuse to believe it. You're lying. I don't know why, I don't know what your game is, but that's not our Whitney. She wouldn't sell drugs, for God's sake." He sat with a thump and squeezed his wife's hand on the table.

Erickson said, "We know how awful this must be for you."

Mr. Chandler glared at Erickson. "You know nothing. Get out of our house. You'll be hearing from our lawyer."

Shelby swallowed. "Mr. and Mrs. Chandler, can you think of any reason Whitney needed money? She didn't have a car. We can't see any evidence of—"

"Like I said," Mr. Chandler bit out. "You'll be hearing from our lawyer." Mrs. Chandler pressed her face into her husband's shoulder, muffling her sobs. He wrapped his arm around his wife and turned his face away, dismissing them.

Shelby and Erickson collected their gear and exited the house. Neither of them said a word as they drove back to the station.

Eleven

Naomi met the detectives at the door to the bullpen. "We put out the BOLO on Bobby Garza."

"Great." Shelby handed the evidence bags to Naomi. "Run these to forensics. We want all the data from the burner phone, but I'm especially interested in any prints they can pull from the box of condoms."

"On it." Naomi strode away, bags in her hand.

In an unspoken agreement, Shelby and Erickson went to the conference room, shutting the door behind them. Shelby stood in the corner, chewing her cheek, while Erickson leaned on the table, palms flat.

"Other than Bobby, and possibly Del," Erickson started, "who else would know where Whitney was getting the drugs?"

"Her customers, maybe. We can use the burner to track them down."

"If we can't do it that way, we'll have to get a warrant for phone records, which will take some time."

Shelby nodded.

Erickson crossed his arms. "So far, based on what forensics told us, the killer was a big male, wearing a red jersey. Could be Bobby Garza—"

"Although, according to Del and everyone else we talked to, that's unlikely."

Erickson narrowed his eyes. He stared at Shelby for a beat, then continued. "Could be Bobby Garza." Shelby pressed her lips into a thin line. "Could be a customer. Could be her supplier."

"Customer seems more likely, don't you think? Someone who wasn't in their right mind. A supplier would be more business minded, I think. Wouldn't want to draw attention or ruin good business in Locust Grove."

He nodded. "Okay. If that's the case then, what? A customer didn't want to pay and got violent? Or was high and didn't realize what they were doing?"

Shelby sighed and shrugged. "Right now, it's all possible."

"I liked it better when Bobby was the only suspect."

Shelby glared at him.

"That look? That look you're giving me? We're going to have a discussion about that." He pointed at her. "In the meantime, we need to follow up with Del, talk to Skye, and start working on that burner phone."

Shelby went to the restroom while Erickson checked his messages. As she washed her hands, she stared at herself in the mirror. She knew she was hiding from her own instincts about Bobby. But her scars were too thick, ran too deep. They kept her from having the same knee-jerk response as Erickson.

By the time they were ready to leave the station, Naomi was back with a sheaf of paper. "The numbers from the burner phone." She was panting slightly.

"Wow." Erickson raised his eyebrows. "Way to light a fire under forensics, Officer Kim." He winked at her. Naomi grinned.

Annoyed, Shelby said, "What about the warrant for Whitney's cellphone records?"

"Oh." Naomi's smile faded. "We're running into delays because she was a minor. The judge needs her parents' sign-off."

Shelby shared a meaningful look with Erickson. "Think we'll get it after what just happened?"

Erickson said, "If they want to find her killer."

Shelby turned to Naomi. "I also want you to sift through her social media accounts. She had a makeshift studio in her room. Maybe she did those confessional kinds of videos and we could learn something. Pull in Officer Simon if you need to."

Naomi gave a firm nod.

"And if you're as fast with that as you were with forensics," Erickson gave the young woman a high-wattage smile, "we'll have this sicko behind bars in no time."

Shelby's jaw ticked. She took the phone numbers from Naomi and shoved the pages into Erickson's chest. "You can look those up on your phone while I drive." She strode to her car in the parking lot, not bothering to wait for Erickson. He hopped in just as she started the engine.

"Where to first?" Erickson buckled up, then pulled out his phone with one hand while he held the list of phone numbers in the other.

"We'll talk to Skye first. Maybe she knows where Bobby might have gone, maybe a secret spot he used to meet Whitney. Then we'll circle back to Del."

He nodded.

Skye Stevens lived in a more upscale neighborhood than Whitney or Bobby, at least by Locust Grove standards. The house was new, with signs of construction along the route and in vacant lots. Freshly planted landscaping surrounded it, just like the other new homes on the street.

Shelby rang the doorbell. Skye answered. Her mahogany hair twisted into a messy bun that sat on the top of her head. She wore a pink velour tracksuit and shimmering lip gloss. Her sharply lined eyes flicked between the detectives.

"Skye?" Shelby raised her eyebrows. "I'm Detective Shelby Reed, and this is—"

"I know who you are." Her slender shoulders heaved on a heavy sigh. "Whitney's parents called my mom and then she told me."

"Okay." Shelby glanced at Erickson. "We'd like to talk to you about Whitney. May we come in?"

Skye walked away, leaving the door open for them to follow.

Erickson gestured for Shelby to go first, muttering, "Teenagers."

Shelby felt the corner of her mouth lift.

The house had an open floor plan, with the kitchen, dining, and living area sharing a large, vaulted space.

Skye waved to one length of a sectional, then curled up on the other, her slippered feet tucked underneath her. "What do you want to know?"

Shelby's eyes scanned the house. It was quiet. "Before we can ask you anything, we need to have one of your parents present. Are either of them home?"

"No." Frustration rose inside Shelby, but dissipated when Skye said, "I'm eighteen. Does that make a difference?"

Shelby met Erickson's eyes. He smiled and tilted his head, giving her the go-ahead.

Shelby took out her notebook and pen. "According to Whitney's parents, you took Whitney to the football game. What time was that?"

Skye squinted. "Like, six? Her parents always want her to eat dinner before the game, so she doesn't gorge on junk food or something." She rolled her eyes.

"Were you with her for the entire game?"

"Yeah, pretty much. We sat together."

Erickson rested his elbows on his knees and clasped his hands together. "Did she go off alone at any point?"

"No. We used the buddy system, just in case." Then the reality of Whitney's death seemed to hit Skye. She paled. "I guess that was pointless, huh?" She blinked as her eyes grew shiny.

"And then the two of you went to Bobby's for the after-party," Shelby said.

Skye twisted a piece of loose hair around her finger. "Yeah. They're not, like, big parties or anything. I mean, you want to party-party, you go to Todd's."

"Todd's?"

"Yeah, Todd Davidson. His parties are fire." Skye widened her eyes. "But like, he's grounded. We haven't been to his place in ages. Anyway, when we're at Bobby's, we all just hang out, decompress and debrief after the games, you know?"

"At any point during the night," Erickson jumped in, "did Whitney fight with Bobby?"

"Or anyone else?" Shelby added.

Skye scrunched up her face. "Ew. No. You think I'd hang out with a bunch of drama llamas? No way."

"Okay." Shelby scribbled in her notebook. "What time did you leave the party?"

One side of Skye's mouth pinched. "About ten forty-five. I wanted to get home by eleven so I could do some SAT prep before bed."

Erickson said, "You're getting ready for the SATs?"

"Took it this morning." Her eyes fell to the cuff of her sweatshirt where she was pulling at the elastic. "Whitney was supposed to be there. I kind of knew something bad must have happened when she didn't show up." She swallowed. "She would never skip out on the SAT."

Shelby said, "We heard you and Whitney were top students, competing for valedictorian."

Skye nodded and looked up again. "Yeah. The SAT has nothing to do with class rank, of course, but I was hoping to get a higher score than Whit. Bragging rights, you know?" She huffed and gave them a fake smile. "Guess I'm valedictorian now. Yay for me. I bet Mr. Long will lose his shit." She brought her hand to her mouth on a gasp. "OMG, I bet he's a wreck over Whitney."

"Mr. Long?" Shelby made a note. "The Quiz Bowl coach?"

Skye's messy bun bounced as she nodded. "Yeah."

Erickson narrowed his eyes. "Why would he be a wreck?"

"Because, like, he's totally in love with Whitney. Or was, I guess."

Both Shelby and Erickson snapped to attention. Skye noticed. "No, no. Not, like, for real. I just mean, like, teacher's pet, y'know? Like, she was his favorite."

The detectives relaxed, but no one had mentioned Long's special relationship with Whitney. New information meant a new lead.

Shelby said, "Did they see each other outside of school?"

Skye scrunched her face. "I don't think so. But during practice, they would go off on their own sometimes, chit chat, and record TikTok dances and stuff."

Shelby looked like someone fed her a whole lemon. "A teacher? Doing TikTok dances? With a student?"

"I know, right?" Skye leaned forward. "It sounds cool, but it was, like, sad, you know?"

"Totally," Erickson said, meeting Shelby's eyes. She underlined Tom Long's name in her notebook.

"Are you dating anyone?" Erickson asked. "Anyone on the football team?"

Skye made a face again. "No. I don't have time for a relationship. I don't know how Whitney kept up her grades and had time for a boyfriend."

"Skye," Shelby said, shifting in her seat. "Did you know Whitney was taking prescription drugs?"

It was like a door slammed shut behind Skye's eyes. "What do you mean?"

Erickson cocked his head. "Del told us that Whitney sometimes took prescription medication to help her study or when she needed to sleep. Did you know that?"

She picked at her cuff again. "Sometimes when we studied together, at night, she took a pill, but she said it was melatonin." Skye's questioning eyes looked up. "That's over-the-counter, right?"

"It is," Shelby answered, "but we don't think she was taking melatonin. Del said she took Adderall and Valium. Maybe more. We don't know."

Skye's jaw dropped. "Whoa. That is so basic. I mean, I knew she wanted to be the best, but..." She trailed off and shook her head. Her back straightened and her jaw stiffened. "Did you know she was selling? I know that. She talked about it. Like, she thought she was bragging, telling me how much money she was making with her little side hustle. I was like, ew. I can't even. But she swore to me she wasn't using." Her lip curled. "What a liar."

Erickson nodded. "We know she was selling. We found her stash. What can you tell us about that?"

Skye pulled her feet under her on the couch. "She said it was for her college fund or whatever, because she wasn't sure if she'd get a scholarship to an Ivy League school. She needed to save up, just in case." Her pink lips formed a tight smile. "I don't have to worry about money for college. No matter what. So I wasn't interested in her little scheme." Her head shook again. "I can't believe she was using. That's cheating." Her eyes glittered.

Shelby could easily see how the girls were friends and enemies at the same time. No one else could relate to their ambition, but that very ambition was a wedge in their friendship. She also figured the difference between Whitney's and Skye's incomes was another source of animosity between them. "Did you ever see her with any of her customers? Or the person who supplied the drugs?"

Erickson added, "Did she ever talk about those people?"

"She didn't say anything about who she sold to. I told her when she started selling to keep it to herself, because I didn't want to be an accessory to a crime or whatever." She threaded the loose piece of hair back into her bun.

Erickson said, "Very smart."

"But there was one guy." Skye grabbed a furry throw pillow and hugged it to her chest. "I always saw them sneaking into empty classrooms or hiding out under the stairs. He must have been a regular."

"He's a student? Do you know his name?" Shelby held her pen ready.

"Danny something." Skye raised a finger. "Hold on." She picked up her phone from the couch. "I can check the school directory."

"We need one of those." Shelby said to Erickson, while she made a note to ask Principal Wheeler for one.

"Here he is." Skye turned the phone so they could see his picture. "Daniel Mendez. He's a senior, too." She tucked her phone away. "Plus, may I just say, he and Whitney looked very cozy together, if you know what I mean." She scrunched up her face. "Which, like, I never understood, because Bobby is hot, and Daniel is not." Again, Skye's eyes flared for emphasis.

Shelby turned to Erickson, whose eyebrows lifted, just like hers. Another new lead.

Twelve

Shelby started her car and backed out onto the street. "Well, that was incredibly enlightening."

Erickson flipped the car's visor down. The autumn sun had strengthened over the day, pushing away the dull clouds that had been hanging over Locust Grove. He said, "Did you get the feeling Skye has no sense of loyalty? Whitney's BFF my ass."

"Well," Shelby said, "in all fairness, Naomi said they were more like frenemies."

He shook his head. "Teenage girls." He turned in Shelby's direction. "I can't picture you ever acting like that."

She ignored his comment. "We'll talk to Tom Long before we track down this Daniel Mendez kid." She cocked her head. "Interesting that not a single person we've talked to has mentioned him."

Erickson nodded. "Looks like Whitney had more than one secret to keep."

The yard around Tom Long's house was scrubby and unruly. Along the edges, the grass was several inches tall, beginning to overtake the driveway and front walk. Brown, bare patches spotted the lawn, while in some places clippings from the last mowing sat in clumps.

"I thought teachers were meticulous people." Erickson kicked a clump of weeds along the walk.

"They're just people." Shelby rang the doorbell and waited. The bright sun cast their reflections on the glass storm door. She noted the frizzy flyaways of hair that had escaped her ponytail, while Erickson looked ready for a photo shoot. She rang again. From inside the house, they heard, "Hang on."

After some bumps and scuffling, footsteps approached the door. It swung open. A middle-aged man with thinning brown hair and puffy bags under his eyes blinked at them. He wore a faded Bellmoor Prep t-shirt, black sweatpants, and a striped robe. Through the glass, he called, "Can I help you?"

Erickson smacked his badge against the glass, holding it in place. Tom Long reared back, as if he'd been punched, his eyes wide.

Shelby said, "We have some questions we'd like to ask you." Long froze, like a rabbit caught in the gaze of a predator. She had an inkling he might slam the door and run, so she said, "About Quiz Bowl and Whitney Chandler." His posture relaxed, and he blew air through his lips, clearly relieved.

Erickson replaced his badge on his belt, and with unmoving lips, whispered, "I hope this guy doesn't play poker."

Long opened the door. "Please, come in. Sorry, you caught me catching up on my sleep." They followed him down the hallway into the kitchen, where the smell of alcohol singed the inside of Shelby's nose. Long grabbed an armful of empty bottles—Wild Turkey, Shelby thought—and tossed them in a recycling bin just outside the back door. "Coffee?" He moved to the stained coffeemaker on the counter and began making a fresh pot. "I know I need a few cups." He forced a breathy laugh.

Shelby retrieved her notebook and pen from her jacket. "Do you mind if we sit?" Four stools stood around the kitchen island, which was covered in scribbled notes, opened envelopes, and various pens and pencils.

"Of course, of course." He waved at the stools while he gathered cups, sugar, and creamer. "You said this was about Quiz Bowl?" He leaned back against the counter, his hands braced on the edges.

"Partly." Shelby shifted on the uncomfortable stool. "We're investigating the murder of Whitney Chandler, and we know she was on your Quiz Bowl team."

His face paled slightly. Whether from a hangover or because they were here to question him about Whitney, Shelby couldn't be sure.

He said, "My son told me what happened. Such a shame. Such a bright girl. Any ideas who killed her?"

"We're running down some leads, still asking questions." Shelby watched him move from foot to foot, as if trying to strike the right pose. "As part of the investigation, we're confirming alibis for the night Whitney was murdered. Where were you Friday night, around midnight?"

The coffee pot sputtered, having finished brewing, but Long ignored it. He blinked at Shelby. "I'm sure Al told you. We were at a hotel in Pittsburgh for a conference."

"He did." Shelby took a note. "Like I said, we're just confirming our information."

Erickson asked, "When did you return to Locust Grove?"

Long turned his back to them, pouring coffee into cups. "How do you want your coffee fixed?"

Shelby's eyes swept the kitchen. "None for me, thank you."

"Two sugars and lots of milk for me," Erickson said. Shelby gave an almost imperceptible shake of her head. Erickson just winked at her.

Long placed their cups in front of them, moving aside the paper detritus, retrieved his own, then joined them at the island. "To be honest, I can't remember. Ten? Eleven? On Saturday morning. The drive home was a bit of a blur." When Shelby's pen paused and leveled him with a stern look, he hurried to say, "Not because I was buzzed. No, no. I was sober. Just had a massive headache, and I've made that drive so many times I kind of go on autopilot."

She nodded and continued writing. "And what about Principal Wheeler?"

"He wasn't far behind me. We went our separate ways Friday night. He said something about getting one last good night's sleep before coming home. You know what it's like with teenagers in the house." Long leaned toward Shelby, apparently assuming she had children.

"No, I don't." She held his gaze and watched as his jovial smile faded.

"Oh, uh." Long's pale face burned red. "I just mean, you can't really go to sleep until they're home, safe and sound, whether it's nine p.m. or two a.m. Once you hear them stomp in and lock the door, then you can finally conk out." He gulped his coffee. "He left the hotel about the same time I did."

Shelby said, "Tell us about Whitney."

His eyes bounced between them. "What do you want to know?"

Erickson stretched his long legs in front of him. He dwarfed the stool, which must have been uncomfortable under his tall frame. "Did she have friends on the team? Did you ever see her with anyone suspicious?"

Long balked at the last question. "Suspicious? Whitney?" He blew breath through his lips like a horse. "Heck, no. Like I said, she was a bright girl. Everyone liked her. The rest of the team looked up to her."

"She was good at the game?" Shelby asked.

"Good?" Long snorted. "The best. Almost had a photographic memory." He frowned. "Or the memory of an elephant. Or both." He drank again. "And quick on the draw, too. That pretty little hand would slap the buzzer before anyone else even thought about it."

Erickson's eyes slid to Shelby's. Yes, she'd caught the "pretty." She said, "And your relationship with her?"

Long's eyes widened a fraction. "What do you mean 'my relationship?' I was her coach."

"Sure." Erickson tried to rest his feet on the rail of the stool, but gave up when his heels didn't fit. "But if she was your best player, you must have had some rapport with her?"

Long smiled, relaxing. "Of course. She was great to work with. Like I said, picked up everything easy-peasy."

Shelby asked, "Did you ever meet with her one on one?"

Long swallowed. "A few times. To go over strategy, talk about the next school we were up against."

Erickson said, "Where did you meet for these one on ones?"

"My classroom."

Erickson nodded. "Never at her house or here at your house. Or someplace else."

Long frowned. "No." He stared at Shelby, then at Erickson. "Our relationship was entirely appropriate for a teacher and a student, if that's what you're getting at."

"Does that include recording TikTok dances with her?" Erickson raised his eyebrows, the corner of his mouth lifting.

Long let out a breathy giggle. "Those were just for fun. You know, trying to meet them where they are. It's hard to connect with kids today." He ran his fingers through his sparse hair, smoothing it against his head. Then they heard footsteps approaching.

A slender teenage boy wearing a flannel and jeans, with his brown hair sticking out in all directions, entered the kitchen, then froze. Long plastered on a smile. "This is my son, Austin." To his son, he said, "These are the detectives looking into Whitney's murder."

Austin took a step towards his father. "Hi." His mouth was full of braces. He turned to his father. "Where's mom?"

"She's at the gym." Long's bloodshot eyes slid from his son's to Shelby's. "Are we finished?"

Shelby flipped to a fresh page. "Just about." She smiled at Austin. "Did you know Whitney?"

Austin's face wore an expression that, to Whitney, was the epitome of teenagers. Tightness around the mouth. Slight wrinkle in the forehead. Absolute disdain in the eyes. He glanced at his father, who nodded his go-ahead. "Yeah."

"Did you like her?"

Austin flushed, and his eyes darted between the adults in the kitchen. "No."

Erickson gave Austin a half smile. "We don't mean, did you like-like her. We mean, was she nice? Were you friends?" Erickson sipped from his mug.

"Oh." Now the kid's face grew redder. He shrugged and dropped his eyes to the floor. "I mean, yeah. She was nice. I didn't really know her." He shot a sideways glance at his father. "Not like Dad did."

Long laughed and squeezed his son's shoulders. "You mean because she's been on the team longer than you?" He leaned toward Shelby and Erickson. "Austin just joined the Quiz Bowl team this year."

Austin shook off his father's hands. "Yeah. That's what I meant." Then he went to the refrigerator and started searching its contents, his back to them.

Long watched him for a moment, then said, "Is that about it? I have papers to grade, and Austin needs to get to a study date." His fingers were white on his coffee mug.

"Dad," Austin whined from the fridge, "don't call it a date."

Long shrugged with a chagrined look. "Study session."

Shelby closed her notebook. "Thank you for your time." She took out a business card and handed it to Long. "If you think of anything that could help with our investigation, let us know." She and Erickson rose from their stools. Long led them from the kitchen to the front door. On their way out, Shelby glanced over her shoulder to see Austin watching them.

Once Long had waved them goodbye and closed the door, Erickson rubbed his backside with both hands. "I do not understand stools."

Shelby laughed. "What's to understand? You sit on them."

He squinted at her as they opened their car doors. "Do you, though? Or are you suspended in air, neither comfortable nor supported?" He slid inside and strapped in. "I feel like people buy stools because they don't want their guests hanging around. If they really wanted people to be comfortable, they would just put out a table and chairs. Christ." He winced and shifted in his seat.

"We're not all monoliths. Some of us do perfectly well sitting on stools." Although, as she pulled into traffic, she couldn't help but think her own backside would have benefited from a cushion.

Thirteen

The sky hung low and grey over the station, a cold, metallic expanse mirroring the mood as Shelby and Erickson arrived. The sun had begun its descent toward the horizon and the breeze held a chilly hint of the winter to come. Before they could shed their jackets, Captain Guerrero pulled them into her office.

"We've got a problem," she said as she shut her door and sat behind her desk. She gestured for the detectives to take a seat.

Erickson removed his jacket as he sat down. "Right here in River City? No, wait. That's trouble."

Shelby took off her jacket as well. "What's going on?"

Guerrero steepled her fingers. "The Chandlers are suing the department for defamation."

"Defamation?" Shelby's brow furrowed. "How can that be?"

Guerrero pursed her lips. "They're saying that you," she nodded at Shelby, then Erickson, "planted drugs in Whitney's room, and now, posthumously, the department is spreading damaging lies about Whitney's character."

Erickson's jaw dropped. "That's insane." He held out his hands as his eyes flitted around the office, as if looking for answers. "Why would we do that? What possible reason would we have? We didn't know the victim. I don't give two shits what kind of girl she was."

Shelby bent, holding her head in her hands while she listened to Erickson, already picturing the roadblocks a lawsuit would throw in their path. "All I care about is investigating her murder." He made a choking sound. "You would think her parents would be more interested in finding her killer than protecting their darling's reputation."

"Careful," Shelby said, lifting her head.

"They're grieving," Guerrero said, holding Erickson's eye. "They're lashing out. We don't have answers for them yet, so they're coming up with their own. It's what people do. They want someone to blame, and until we know who killed Whitney, we're the target of their pain."

Shelby shrugged. "Their suit won't hold up, anyway. The truth is on our side. We have fingerprints. We have witnesses."

Guerrero's eyes softened. "I know. I feel for them. I really do." She leaned back in her chair. "But in the meantime, it's bad optics for us, especially when we need the community on our side to get answers. People already distrust us. Now we're tainting the angelic reputation of Bellmoor Prep's star student."

Erickson gripped the arms of his chair. "Now, every time we knock on someone's door, they're going to hide behind their curtains. They'll think we're going to haul them in on made-up charges."

"Or," Guerrero clasped her hands in her lap, "they won't say anything for fear of being wrong or spreading rumors."

Shelby looked at her partner, then her captain. "I don't think so. So far, it seems like people loved Whitney. They want justice for her. And, in my experience," she clasped her hands in her lap, "people in small towns are always looking for their fifteen minutes of fame. They might be more willing to talk than you're giving them credit."

"Either way, we need to solve this case and put it to rest." Guerrero stood and opened her office door, dismissing the detectives. "When we do that, the Chandlers will have no choice but to drop their suit. Now, get out there and do your jobs. I have to call the chief and explain that my detectives absolutely did not plant evidence at a crime scene." Her lips pressed into a thin line as she shut her door behind them.

A thunder cloud hung over Erickson as they entered the conference room, now their makeshift office. He fixed a cup of stale coffee and threw himself into a seat, brooding.

Shelby studied him. "First time someone accused you of being a crooked cop?"

"No." He sipped his coffee, grimaced, then set the cup on the table. "Yes. I mean, I've had low-lifes swear at me and accuse me of all kinds of things. But never anything official like this." His fingers drummed the table. "The Chandlers better not screw up this investigation for me." Shelby raised an eyebrow. "For us. For Whitney. We need to catch this killer." He stubbed his forefinger against the tabletop, emphasizing his point. "Before he kills again." He took another swig of his coffee, forgetting how bad it was, grimaced, then threw it in the trash. "How dare they think we would plant evidence?"

Shelby slowly nodded and took a seat a few chairs away from Erickson. "It smarts. I know."

He narrowed his eyes. "You've been sued before?"

"No. Nothing like that." She swallowed, fighting the urge to spill her guts. Erickson was proving to be a decent detective, but she needed to stay professional, maintain boundaries. Heat prickled at the back of her neck. A partial truth wouldn't hurt. "I've been called out in the court of public opinion. It's painful, especially when you take pride in your work, dotting every i, crossing every t."

A corner of Erickson's mouth lifted, and he tilted his head comically. "Making sure you don't beat the living shit out of the assholes you put in cuffs."

She chuckled. "Something like that."

He slumped a little, tracing an invisible pattern on the table with his finger. "How did you deal with it?"

Images of her late husband flashed through her mind, of his stroking her hair, squeezing her hand, gathering her onto his lap. She took in a deep breath. "I stayed focused on the case, pushed the noise away. Because all that noise won't help us find the killer."

He pursed his lips and nodded. "Easier said than done." He scrunched up his face, looking at the ceiling. "I was hoping your answer had something to do with cases of beer or a punching bag."

She laughed. "A punching bag sounds good."

He pretended to survey the room. "We could hang one in the corner. Pin the lawsuit to it."

"Yeah, we could."

Will appeared, leaning through the door. His hair, which was usually styled to the latest trend's perfection, was mussed. "Detectives, got a sec?"

"Sure," Shelby answered.

"Naomi and I have been combing Whitney's social media. She's mostly active on TikTok."

"What did you find?"

Nodding appreciatively, he said, "The girl had moves." After a look from Shelby, he sobered. "Most of her videos were dance trends or rants about getting into college, how expensive college is, that kind of thing."

Erickson's brow furrowed. "She ever talk about Bobby or Del? Or Skye?"

"Or Tom Long?" Shelby added.

"No." Will tried to smooth his hair. "But Tom Long is in a couple of videos with her."

That confirmed what Skye had told them.

Will straightened his shirt and cleared his throat. "And I have more news. Forensics said the only prints on the drug packets and pill bottles you found are Whitney's."

Erickson couldn't suppress his mischievous smile any longer. He smiled. "Forensics, huh? Been spending a lot of time in forensics?" He turned to Shelby. "Now, who all's in that department?"

Shelby rubbed her chin. "I think there's someone named Shane." She knew Shane and liked him. She also knew he'd broken up with his boyfriend recently.

"Yeah." Erickson clasped his hands behind his head. "The new guy. Looks like Timothée Chalamet."

Will's face turned red as a tomato. "Yeah, Shane. He just called me down to tell me about the, uh, prints." His voice trailed off.

Shelby bit down on her bottom lip to keep from laughing. She had suspected Will had a crush on the recent hire, who was very handsome. Apparently, Shane reciprocated his attraction. She was thankful their attachment was the captain's problem, not hers. "Thank you for the info, Officer Simon."

His head jerked in a nod, and he nearly ran to his desk. Shelby shook her head as Erickson burst into giggles.

Fourteen

"This has to be the best chicken parm I've ever had." Erickson's cheeks were full of his dinner as he chewed. He made obscene sounds as his eyes closed.

Shelby glowered at him, then took a bite of her grilled chicken Caesar salad. "Mario's is the best Italian food in the tri-state area." She glanced at her watch, remembering her father's text from earlier. If she didn't love her little brother so much, she would skip his party and focus on the case. But she did love him. However, her timing tonight had to be perfect. Late enough to avoid most of the guests, but not so late that she seemed rude.

"I've heard that, but never been here." Erickson cut another slice of chicken. "I'll come back to this place; that's for sure. Five stars, easily." He shoved the slice into his mouth, humming again.

They had eaten little during the day, only snacking at the station while they chased down the numbers from Whitney's burner phone. Every single one of them had been disconnected, which meant filing more warrants and more leg work. The warrant for Whitney's cell-phone records was still delayed. With nothing to go on and Bobby still missing, they'd stopped for dinner.

Watching Erickson's eyes fall shut while he ate, Shelby let out a slow breath. Erickson seemed to be a good detective, but his personality was too big for her taste. She used to have a bigger personality, saying what was on her mind and disregarding the consequences. She'd believed in a black and white world of right and wrong, with the edges defined in sharp contrast. Then her world shattered, and she became smaller, quieter. Learned to keep her thoughts to herself unless they were absolutely correct, keeping any and all consequences in mind. Although Erickson had as much experience as she did, he hadn't learned the same lesson. Hadn't needed to.

She was only halfway through her salad when Erickson mopped up the last of the sauce on his plate with a piece of garlic bread. "I didn't realize you were so hungry. You should have said something."

"I was fine." He shrugged. "I love to eat. And I work out pretty hard every morning so I can keep eating." He patted his abs. "The football team had a strict schedule for workouts. It stuck with me after I graduated."

Shelby eyed his strong shoulders and chest, his trim torso. His workout routine served him well. "Good thing, with all the calories you consume." She took another bite of her salad.

He laughed. "You only live once, Reed." He leaned back in his chair. "Next move?"

"Finding Daniel Mendez, that kid Skye mentioned. See what he has to say. Maybe upgrade Bobby's BOLO to an APB."

Erickson nodded. "We could also hit up all of Bobby's friends, teammates. See if we can shake him loose."

She shook her head. "Short of driving up and down every street with a spotlight, it will be hard to find him at night. We know where Mendez lives. We'll go there next."

He dabbed at his mouth with a napkin. "Why do you deflect every time I bring up Bobby?" He pointed over her shoulder, toward the street. "That kid is out there, hiding from us. The only reason he would do that is because he has something to hide. I'm guessing he's hiding because he killed Whitney or knows who did." Now his finger pointed at her. "I think you know that. I think your gut is telling you it's

Bobby, but for some reason you haven't shared with me, you want to look everywhere else. Why? Do you know something I don't? Because we're partners, and that's not how this works."

"I don't know anything you don't." She set her fork down. Her pulse picked up, and she took a deep breath. "My first big case went sideways because I didn't cover all my bases. I won't let that happen again."

Surprise showed on Erickson's face. "What happened? Perp got off on a technicality?"

She shook her head. "No. He was convicted."

Understanding softened his features. "I see. Put the wrong guy away."

She shook her head again. "No, he was the right guy."

His eyebrows pinched as he stared at her. "I'm confused. How did it go sideways if—"

"It was a circus, okay?" She rested her palms on the white table-cloth. "The local and national news picked up the story and turned up the pressure on all of us. Every move we made became a hundred times more difficult with so many eyes on us, questioning everything we did. This case," she pressed her forefinger into the table, "has the potential to become headline news. So, before we hang a teenaged boy out to dry, I want to make absolutely certain we're doing the right thing. Because guilty or not, his life will never be the same."

Her chest rose and fell as her breath picked up. A flush colored her cheeks. Erickson watched with a wary look as Shelby transformed from a stern detective into a fiery advocate. He looked away, then met her eyes. "I'm sorry you were shoved into the spotlight. That doesn't mean it will happen again."

She leaned forward. "Don't you remember the Shepard case?"

He stared at her in confusion, shaking his head. "No."

"A couple of years ago?"

"No." He continued to shake his head. "I was busy climbing the ranks and helping my parents sell plots of land and move to Florida. Hell, I rarely caught a Penguins game on TV, let alone the news."

"Well," she fidgeted with the tablecloth pooled in her lap, "if you had, you'd understand."

"It's not our job to worry about the news or someone's reputation or to keep up appearances."

Tension stretched across the table between them, through the silence.

Shelby said, "It has to be. We can't leave a path of destruction behind us in the name of the law. People will remember. Hell, the Chandlers have already sued our department."

"A young girl is dead." Erickson leaned forward, raising his voice.

Shelby glanced at the other diners, who were sneaking looks at them over their plates. "Erickson, keep your voice down."

He ignored her. "Our job is to track down and bring in her killer. Period. Let the PR department worry about what's left behind. And trust me, the thing people will remember? Is whether we bring Whitney's killer to justice. That's what people care about. That's what they'll remember."

"You don't understand," Shelby said again through gritted teeth.

Erickson laughed without humor. "No. I don't." He spread his arms wide, attracting even more attention in the restaurant. "So, make me understand. Spell it out for me."

Shelby's face burned. When she met the eyes of a woman at the next table, she didn't see shock or curiosity. She saw sadness, sympathy. The woman probably thought they were a couple having an argument. Her breath caught in her chest. The aromas of tomato, oregano, and basil choked her, turned her stomach.

She rose so quickly from her chair that the tablecloth caught under her elbow and slid toward her. Her salad nearly crashed to the floor, but she fumbled it back onto the table. "The uniforms are out looking for Bobby. We focus on Mendez. End of discussion." She grabbed her jacket and purse and flew out of the restaurant, leaving Erickson and half of her salad behind.

The chilly night air cooled her blazing cheeks and scraped her lungs. She sucked in a deep breath, tears threatening to fall. The last thing she wanted was to tell Erickson her full story, to expose her greatest failure.

She massaged her scalp. A throbbing headache was forming like a tight band around her head. She dug through her purse and found a bottle of Tylenol, popping two caplets.

Her phone lit up with the station's number. She exhaled and answered. "Detective Reed."

"Detective, it's Naomi."

"Hey, Naomi. What's up?"

"We have confirmation of the prints taken from the box of condoms you found in Whitney's room."

Shelby heard the door to the restaurant open and close. Heavy footsteps came straight toward her until Erickson stood in front of her. She pointed to her phone and said to Erickson, "The box of condoms." Erickson tipped his chin in understanding. She said to Naomi, "I'm assuming they found Whitney's prints."

"They did." Naomi hesitated. "And another set."

Erickson, who could hear Naomi, asked, "Bobby's?"

"No," Naomi answered. "The only other set of fingerprints on the box of condoms belongs to Daniel Mendez. Turns out he's got a juvie record, so his prints were in the database."

"Officer Kim, get an address for Mendez. We'll need to question him." Shelby ended the call and slipped her phone back into her pocket.

Erickson used his thumb to wipe a dot of sauce from the corner of his mouth. "Mendez, huh? I wonder if Bobby knew about Whitney's extracurricular time with Mendez.."

"Me, too." Shelby looked at her watch. "Unfortunately, it's getting late. We can pick this up tomorrow."

Erickson paused with his hand on the handle of the passenger side of Shelby's car. "What? Why? Let's bring in Mendez and question him. Maybe by then we'll have a lead on Bobby's whereabouts."

Shelby slid into the driver's side and started the car. "I can't. I have a family commitment I can't get out of." After Erickson buckled his seatbelt, she pulled out into traffic. "Trust me, I'd rather go back to the station and work this case. I'll drop you there on my way. Can you get a ride home?"

"Getting a ride home isn't the problem." He rolled his head, like his neck was stiff. "The problem is we have a murderer to find, and the Chandlers filed a lawsuit against us. Clock's ticking, Reed."

"I know that." Shelby chewed her tongue. "But I don't go back on my commitments. Why don't you follow up on some of those phone records and check the videos again? I'll pick you up again tomorrow, bright and early."

She pulled into the police station and let her engine idle. The station's vestibule lighting, visible through the front door's window, was dim and sallow in the dark, which came early this time of year.

Erickson undid his seatbelt. "For the record, no one who knows me would expect me to show up for a party while I'm working a case."

As he climbed out of the car, Shelby leaned forward and caught his eye. "For the record, you're lucky you have people like that in your life." He shut the door and strode into the station. She backed up and turned away before the door closed.

Fifteen

Shelby had to park her car twenty yards from her father's driveway. Enough cars lined the street that parking was tight. Fairy lights, strung over every tree and shrub in the perfectly landscaped yard, glinted off the high-end SUVs and sedans. Not a grimy one among them.

Music and laughter met her ears as she neared the massive brick house her father, Mark Reed, had bought after he married her stepmother. The house was a mishmash of arches, pillars, dormers, and tall windows. It wasn't inviting, but it was impressive. And Chandra, her stepmother, was all about being impressive.

Yard signs festooned with balloons and streamers led her to the sprawling backyard, complete with an outdoor kitchen and bar, pergola, swimming pool, and sauna. Her father made good money as the county's district attorney, good enough for the mini estate they'd built and the lavish vacations they took. Chandra quit her job as a clerk at the courthouse when she had Kavi, Shelby's half-brother.

The only familiar faces in the crowd of laughing, drinking guests were her father, mixing drinks at the bar, her stepmother, entertaining in the Adirondack chairs around the fire pit, and Kavi, playing volleyball with his friends. Shelby gripped the small gift bag in her hand and pushed her way to the bar.

When her father spotted her, he called out to her while he contin-ued mixing someone's drink. His silver hair was slicked back, his face tanned from hours spent on the golf course. She leaned her elbow on the bar while her father finished. He said, "Chad, you remember my daughter?"

Chad turned bleary eyes on her. This wasn't his first drink. Or his second. "I sure do. Still as pretty as you were when you were in high school." He gave her a lopsided smile.

Shelby gave him a tight one in return.

"Brains and beauty," her father said. "She's a detective, you know."

Chad raised his eyebrows. "That's right. Any hot cases?" He leaned toward her, the alcohol on his breath scorching the hairs in her nose.

Before she could say anything, her father answered. "Got one right now. Maybe you saw it on the news? Found a young girl dead at the bottom of a pool."

"Raped?" Chad asked. She and her father shared a guarded look while Chad waited.

Shelby gave Chad the answer she gave everyone who craved sala-cious details from the cases she worked. "I can't comment on an ongo-ing investigation."

Chad scoffed, while her father let his eyes drift back to the cocktail in his hands. He didn't drink at social gatherings. As a district attor-ney, he couldn't afford to have a loose tongue.

As he handed Chad his drink, Shelby said, "I'm going to say hi to Chandra."

"Meet you over there."

No one looked twice at Shelby as she wound her way through the crowd of strangers. They were decked out in high-end outerwear, while she still wore her pantsuit and frizzy ponytail. As she reached Chandra, her soft cardigan wrapped around her tightly, Shelby caught her conversation with a slim brunette seated sideways on the next re-cliner. "Brooke, I swear, if that bag was the real deal, then I don't know Gucci from garbage."

Brooke laughed, pointing a manicured finger at Chandra. "And you know Gucci."

Chandra noticed Shelby. "Shelby! You made it." She tucked her feet under her tiny body and patted the seat of an empty chair. "Brooke, this is my stepdaughter Shelby."

Brooke's mouth dropped. "I didn't know you had a stepdaughter." Her eyes raked over Shelby while Shelby felt a familiar ache, like a fist was squeezing her heart. Her old resentments bubbled up, but she pressed her lips into the semblance of a smile. Of course, Chandra's friend didn't know she had a stepdaughter. Shelby was sure Chandra never talked about her, only spending breath on her dear Kavi. Brooke playfully tapped Chandra's shoulder. "I bet you make a divine wicked stepmother." The two of them cackled.

Chandra's finely plucked eyebrows pulled together. "Shelby, are you okay? You look tired." She ran her palm up and down Shelby's arm in a motherly way, but Chandra was only a handful of years older than Shelby. The gesture was for Brooke's benefit.

"I'm fine." She lifted the gift bag. "I brought this for Kavi."

Brooke stood. "I'm off to find Luke. Nice to meet you, Shelly." She walked away. Shelby didn't bother to correct her. Brooke would forget her before the party ended.

Chandra swung her legs to the side of the chair. "I think Kavi's still playing volleyball." She tilted her head. "Mark told me you're working on another rough case." Sympathy pulled the corners of her mouth down.

Shelby looked at her stepmother. Chandra's smooth, dark skin glowed even in the falling night. Her sleek, black hair fell smooth over her shoulders. Her onyx, almond-shaped eyes filled with concern. Chandra was beautiful. Her father marrying Chandra hadn't surprised Shelby. She had been surprised he married Chandra less than a year after a drunk driver killed her mother. Shelby had been in college. Her father and Chandra hadn't invited her to the wedding. Only Chandra's family attended. Her father had said he thought it would have been too painful for Shelby. It was all too painful for Shelby, but they didn't seem to notice.

"I am. It's keeping me busy, but I wanted to wish Kavi a happy birthday. You don't turn sixteen every day." She didn't hold a grudge against Kavi. He was a good kid. Her father's slights weren't his fault.

"That's the truth." Her father appeared and took Brooke's vacated seat and handed a glass of white wine to Chandra. "And it's not every day you get inducted into the National Honor Society."

"Did he?" Shelby smiled, genuinely happy for Kavi, who worked his butt off at school.

"He sure did. A year earlier than most kids, too. He's really something." Mark leaned sideways, peering past Shelby to watch Kavi spike the volleyball, a wide smile on his face.

Had her father ever praised Shelby so lavishly? She wasn't sure.

"I was just asking Shelby," Chandra said, "about the recent case you told me about."

The smile vanished from her father's face as he brought his eyes back to Shelby's. "Are you being careful?" He narrowed his eyes. "You can't make any mistakes like, well, like last time."

Shelby drew a breath in through her nose and gripped the edge of the recliner. "I didn't make any mistakes."

Her father lifted his eyebrows while Chandra sipped her wine. "You know what I mean. The media is relentless and unforgiving. Once they sniff out this new case--"

"I've got it." She forced a smile. "Really, I'm on top of it. My partner and I--"

"Guerrero brought in a partner for you?" He nodded and pointed his finger in her direction. "Smart. You shouldn't handle this alone."

Shelby stared at her father for a moment. Did he mean "shouldn't" or "couldn't?" Chandra reached out and placed a hand on his knee. He gave her a warm smile.

Shelby said, "Speaking of the case, I need to get going. Just give this to Kavi."

"Oh, no. Wait a second." Chandra stood. "He'll be devastated if he doesn't get to see you."

Shelby also stood. She didn't think her premature departure would devastate him, but guilt tugged at her gut. She waited.

Chandra waved at Kavi in the pool and called his name. He spotted her, batted away the volleyball, and pushed himself out of the pool. Like most boys his age, he had the gangly walk of someone who was growing faster than his brain could keep up. He was as handsome as his mother was beautiful, although his smile was their father's. "What's up?"

Chandra squeezed his arm. "Shelby wanted to give you your gift before she left."

His eyes lit up. "Hey, Shelby. Thanks for coming."

"No problem. Happy birthday." She handed him the gift bag.

He pulled out a West Virginia University Mountaineers keychain and a Sheetz gift card for fifty dollars. "Awesome. Thank you." He beamed at her, his perfect smile bright in the night.

"I figured you can use the gift card now and hold on to the keychain until you have your own wheels someday." She returned his smile, fondness misting her eyes.

Her father rose from his seat, barking a laugh. "Oh, he doesn't have to wait. We gave him his birthday gift this morning. It's parked in the driveway."

Shelby's insides disappeared. "You got him a car? Already?" When Shelby turned sixteen, her father told her, in no uncertain terms, that life didn't hand you anything. If she wanted a car, she needed to earn it. She worked as a grocery store cashier for two years, socking away every penny, until her father matched what she'd saved. Her beat-up hatchback lasted through college and part of her time as a uniform. She plastered on a smile and turned to Kavi. "What'd you get? I hope it's all-wheel drive if you're headed to WVU in two years."

Kavi chuckled. "It's all-wheel drive, for sure. Mom and Dad got me a BMW X5." Shelby bit the inside of her cheek. A BMW at sixteen.

"Nothing but the best for my son." Her father squeezed Kavi's shoulder. He and Chandra beamed at the boy. Then her father leaned into the boy and whispered, "Did you know Shelby failed her driving test the first time?"

Kavi's eyes went wide. "No way."

Her father chuckled. "Yep. Couldn't parallel park. Can you imagine a police officer failing their driving test?" He turned his laughing face toward her. "Good thing that wasn't part of the interview, right, Shelbs?"

She ignored her father and hugged Kavi. "Congratulations, kid." Her phone buzzed in her pocket. It was Erickson. She was partly grateful for the interruption, and partly annoyed. He knew she was on personal time. "I have to take this. Have a good night." She swiped to answer, sent a casual wave over her shoulder, and walked to the front of the house. The new BMW sat in the driveway. "Erickson."

"How's your party?"

Shelby almost told him the truth, that it was horrible, humiliating, painful as always. Instead, she said, "Fine. Why are you calling? Is there a break in the case?"

"Not really." She heard what sounded like ice clinking in a glass. "But I ran into the captain at the station. She handed me a bunch of anonymous tips that have come in."

She ran her finger over the BMW's shiny hood ornament. "Anything good?"

"Mostly conspiracy theories about a local pizza shop and human trafficking. Oh, and there was one that mentioned Big Foot."

Shelby chewed her lip. "Erickson, this could have waited until tomorrow." More ice clinking. Was he drinking?

"There was one tip I thought you might be interested in." She leaned against the new car, suddenly exhausted. "They claimed Bobby wasn't home the night of Whitney's death."

She rubbed her forehead. "It's an anonymous tip. No one we can interview to verify their information. Why are you telling me?"

"Because." He paused. "Where is he? He wouldn't run if he were innocent."

Sixteen

The next morning, Shelby was out of sorts. Instead of tying up threads in their investigation, they were finding new ones. And the short, but bitter, visit with her family also left her feeling like her guts had unspooled. She needed grounding.

A cloud of purring fur appeared, obscuring her view of her bedroom. Queenie, the cat she rescued from a crime scene—murder-suicide—a year ago, stood on her chest, glaring at Shelby with a clear message in her golden eyes. *Time for my breakfast.*

After feeding Queenie, she showered, had a quick breakfast of black coffee and a protein bar, and left more food and fresh water for Queenie. Out on the road, she pointed her car upwards, taking a steep, one-lane road to a high bluff above the Ohio river.

Sturdy, gray stones bracketed the iron gate of Hilltop Memorial Gardens. A weak sun gilded the red and orange leaves that lined the drive and shone in dappled puddles on the asphalt. Shelby maneuvered her car slowly around the bend, parking in front of the community mausoleum.

Yesterday had been exhausting. Shelby had tossed and turned all night, dreaming of blonde hair that spread over murky water like seaweed, and dark figures appearing in the corner of her eye, only to vanish when she looked at them directly. Then she was chasing a faceless football player in a red and white jersey down shadowy streets. She raced around a corner only to come to a screeching halt, the faceless boy holding a revolver pointed right at her.

When she woke, her first thought was to visit Hilltop Memorial Gardens.

She didn't like the practice of naming cemeteries as gardens, as if the dead had been planted and would sprout from the earth. Calling it a park, as some cemeteries were named, wasn't much better. Why wasn't it just called a cemetery? Even burial ground was better.

At least her husband wasn't lying underground, decaying. He would have hated that.

After her husband died, she'd been thankful the two of them had spoken about how they wanted to be interred. They'd been on their honeymoon in Cozumel, naked in the afterglow of a lovely, lazy coupling, her chin resting on her forearms over his chest. Their conversation had drifted from one topic to another, as it does when you're a newlywed, living in a romantic bubble with no schedule nipping at your heels. They'd talked about a variety of things, from subjects as trivial as whether sandwiches tasted better with sliced avocado or guacamole, to topics as weighty as the death penalty. At one point, they'd talked about whether they wanted to be buried or cremated when they died.

"Cremated, for sure," Shawn had said. "Probably interred back home in Locust Grove. My parents have plots, but I want to be cremated."

She had smiled as she drew a lazy figure eight in his chest hair. "I was going to say the same thing." She'd tilted her head to see his face. "What's your reason?"

He'd run his hand over her tangled hair. "It's kind of macabre." He'd rolled his eyes.

She'd laughed and slid onto her side, using his firm stomach as a pillow. His eyes had turned bashful. "Tell me. I won't think it's macabre." She emphasized the word with her best impression of Vincent Price and crisscrossed her bare breasts with her finger. "I promise."

"Okay." He'd trailed his fingers up and down her arm, leaving goosebumps in their wake. He'd taken a deep breath. "I don't like the idea that we're filling up the Earth with dead bodies." His eyes had met hers, checking her reaction. She'd stared back at him. "Our planet is already overcrowded. Is it going to be, like, one day there are headstones everywhere you look? I mean, have you seen pictures of Edinburgh?" She'd shaken her head, feeling his body hair graze her cheek. "There's no more room in their graveyards, so they doubled up." His eyes had been as wide as silver dollars. "Can you imagine? And," He'd twisted a strand of her hair around his finger, giving her delicious tingles. "They've actually used some headstones as part of the walls of churches and other buildings. Like, built onto them, because there wasn't any room." He wrinkled his nose. "It grosses me out. And this earth is for the living, not the dead. Why should graves take up all that glorious green space?" He swallowed and played with a corner of the bedspread. "Isn't that silly? I mean, it would take hundreds, maybe thousands, of years before we run out of room, but it bothers me." His hand gently squeezed her hip.

"I don't think it's silly." She'd taken his hand and kissed it, then held it against her heart.

"Why not?"

"Because it's how you feel." She'd placed a soft kiss on his torso. "Your feelings will never be silly to me. I will always be on your side. Forever."

His eyes had softened as he'd pulled her up the bed, kissing her deeply, time stretching to accommodate their overwhelming affection. "I love you."

"I love you, too."

The memory faded, swept away like the dead leaves skittering in the breeze around her feet.

Shelby walked across the small parking lot and down the narrow lane to the lawn opposite the mausoleum. The cemetery bore the name Hilltop because of its location, literally at the top of a hill that rose above Locust Grove. A sharp drop-off ran along the edge of the cemetery, a rocky hillside falling straight down to Route 2 and the Ohio River. Although trees stood sentinel along the edge, Shelby had a clear view of the river winding its way between hills, past the steel mill, and along the road below. Not for the first time, she marveled that such a beautiful piece of property was dedicated to the dead, who couldn't fully appreciate the view.

The river was steely gray, bordered by two gray asphalt highways. The mill was gray. So was the sky that stretched for miles in each direction. She used to love the bright colors of the fall, but this pewter environment was more comforting. No pops of color demanding her attention. She only had so much attention to go around, and it was focused on this case.

Shelby retraced her steps, then opened the heavy metal doors of the mausoleum, which stood in the center of the cemetery. Although the watery sun shone through the windows that stretched from floor to ceiling at the end of the central corridor, the marble walls kept the interior chilly year-round. As a police officer, Shelby had visited far too many morgues. Every time she visited the mausoleum, she tried not to think of refrigerated drawers and toe tags, but the cool temperature inside made it difficult.

Hilltop Memorial Gardens had been there for decades, so the choicest spots had been taken when Shawn died. The days after his death were a blur of interviews, paperwork, phone calls, and decisions she hadn't prepared for, including planning Shawn's service and interment. By the time she'd met with Shawn's parents in Locust Grove, Shelby had chosen cremation for Shawn and the community mausoleum, as well as a short, secular service, and a luncheon at their home afterwards. They had been taken aback that she'd made all the decisions without them. But they'd been allowed to see Shawn one last time, to say goodbye, before his cremation, and that seemed to settle them. After that, they'd been an enormous comfort and help.

Shelby crouched in front of Shawn's square of marble, in the last corridor to the left, the second row from the bottom. She ran her fingers over the small bronze plaque that bore his name, Shawn Ingram. When Shelby had told Shawn she wanted to keep her maiden name, he'd said, "Of course. You should. I didn't expect anything different." It had been another click of the lock on her heart, deepening her love for him.

"Hey, sweetheart." Although her voice was barely more than a whisper, it bounced off the marble all around her.

She didn't visit the mausoleum often. She didn't need to. Her mind offered up memories of him all day, every day that kept him close to her. She visited when she needed reassurance, grounding. It was a peaceful place.

"I have a new partner. His name is Jasper Erickson. Can you believe that? I never thought I'd meet someone named Jasper. Sounds like a cartoon character. Kind of acts like one." Her eyes roamed the corridor, catching on a bouquet of burgundy mums placed in a brass vase next to someone else's square of marble. "You'd like him. You'd appreciate his jokes." Shelby huffed. "I'm learning to. I'd like him to take the case more seriously." Someone else's bouquet of sunflowers and daisies was brown and crispy. She chewed her lip. "I think I'm letting my feelings cloud my judgement. At least, that's what Jasper says." She blew out a breath. "Who am I kidding? Of course, I am. I guess I'm thankful he's been here to call me on it." Her eyes narrowed, picturing Erickson's piercing brown eyes. "He sees through my bullshit. Just like you did." Her finger traced the outline of Shawn's name. "I'm not the same person I used to be. I just want to feel like me again, you know?" Her lips lifted in a weak smile. "I need you for that, though, don't I? I don't know how to be me without you." She rested her hand on the cold marble. "I guess I better figure it out. I know you'd want me to."

She stood, a little stiff after crouching in the chill. The corridor darkened as a cloud drifted across the sun. The bouquets turned black in the shadow.

Back outside, she shoved her hands into her coat pockets. Without the sun's warmth, the day turned brisk.

Over the roof of her car, Shelby spotted movement at the end of the drive, where headstones lay flat against the ground, creating a seamless view of green. A woman clutched a tissue to her face, while a man kept his arm around her waist. Another man clasped his hands in front of him, talking to the couple. When he gestured to the ground, she realized he must be the cemetery's manager, pointing out a burial location. As she watched, the man and woman lifted their heads, nodding. An icy finger ran down her spine. It was the Chandlers, Whitney's parents.

All too well, she remembered coming here to see where Shawn would rest for eternity. How she had tried to function like a normal human being while her entire world had shattered, daily life seeming frivolous and foreign. Her heart broke for them, knowing what lay ahead.

"So tragic."

Shelby startled at the voice behind her. She turned to find Skye Stevens staring at the Chandlers, too. She wore a dark wool overcoat, chunky black heels, black stockings, and a dark wool beret. The girl looked like she had stepped out of an Instagram post. "I mean, look at poor Mr. and Mrs. Chandler. It's like a scene in a movie, you know?" In full makeup today, Skye turned large, shadowed eyes on Shelby.

"What are you doing here, Skye?"

"I know, right? Like, why am I hanging out in a cemetery? Gross." She grimaced. "Whitney's parents wanted me to meet them here to talk about, I don't know, a memorial service?"

Shelby glanced back at the Chandlers. The manager was walking them through a section of larger headstones. She was thankful they hadn't spotted her. "You're going to be part of the service?"

"Yeah." Skye tucked a flyaway piece of hair behind her ear. "Read a Bible verse or something. Me and Bobby."

Shelby gave Skye her full attention. "Bobby? Have they spoken with him? Have you?"

Skye wrinkled her nose. "No. He and I weren't besties, you know? I don't think they've spoken to him yet, either, because they want me to send him the info after we talk today." She rolled her eyes. "It's going to be so sad, you know? I wish they'd ask someone else."

"I thought Whitney was your friend." Shelby watched the girl closely.

Skye's eyes widened, and her lips parted. "Oh, I totally am. Was. Whatever." She flapped her hand. "I just mean, this is a crucial time in the college application process. Whitney dying kind of, like, tightened my schedule?" She straightened and crossed her arms in front of her, bracing against the wind. "But I'll do whatever Mr. and Mrs. Chandler need me to do. I won't bail on them. Not when they need me most."

Shelby pressed her lips together. Skye was the star in her own tragedy, regardless of Whitney's death and the Chandlers' grief. She said, "We spoke to Mr. Long."

Alarm filled Skye's eyes. "You didn't tell him I said anything, did you?"

"No." Shelby shoved her hands in her coat pockets. She needed to leave before the Chandlers saw her. The last thing she wanted was to listen to questions that didn't have answers, or defend herself against their accusations. "But he said there was nothing unusual about his relationship with Whitney."

Skye shrugged. "Whatever. He's creepy. Not as creepy as before, but still creepy."

"Before what?"

A wicked grin spread over Skye's face. "Before he got caught slobbering all over Miss Pugh in her car." She wrinkled her nose. "So gross."

"And then he wasn't creepy?" Shelby shook her head.

"Well." Skye rested her fingertips on her shoulder, striking a graceful pose. "See, it was Mr. Wheeler who found them. And when he dragged Mr. Long from the car, I guess he was wasted. Mr. Wheeler put him on probation and said if he was ever drunk on school property again, he'd be fired." She leaned into Shelby for the last sentence, a gleam in her eye.

Shelby cocked her head. "How do you know all this?"

Skye waved her hand. "Everyone knows. See, Mr. Wheeler was blabbing on the phone about it to somebody official, I don't know." She waved her hand again. "And Don Jr. heard him, heard every word. Of course, he told everyone about it the next day. I mean, it really upped his rep, you know?" She chuckled. "Didn't win Don Jr. any points at home, either."

Shelby frowned. "Don Jr.?"

"Oh, Mr. Wheeler's son." Skye shrugged. "He's not really a junior, obvi." She rolled her eyes again. "But we just call him that because he's, like, the principal's son." When Shelby said nothing, Skye said, "Like the president's son? Don Jr.?"

Shelby nodded. "Got it. So, you're saying Mr. Long is currently on probation?"

"Oh, yeah. At school and at home, if you know what I mean." Skye wiggled her eyebrows.

Shelby ignored Skye's snark. "And now that he's on probation, he's not creepy?"

Skye straightened her beret. "Not as, but still a little. I think that's why he was all up on Whitney."

"Why?" Shelby couldn't follow her train of thought. If he wasn't acting as creepy as he had been, why would he still be interested in a student?

"Because she was everyone's favorite? Especially Mr. Wheeler's. So, like, if he and Whitney were tight, then Mr. Wheeler wouldn't fire him, you know?"

"Right." Shelby glanced over her shoulder again and saw the Chandlers walking toward the parking lot. "Thanks, Skye. You've been very helpful."

The girl patted her beret in place. "It's what I do."

The clouds cleared, and the sun burned in the sky again, warming her face. She climbed into her car and drove away, leaving Skye bathed in a ray of light, looking like an angel.

Seventeen

Shelby's phone rang just as she accepted a hot coffee from the boy at the McDonald's drive-through. She placed it in her cup holder and pulled into an empty parking space. She swiped to answer. "Detective Reed."

"Detective, sorry to call so early." Naomi's voice was a little breathless.

"Never too early during an investigation, Naomi. What can I do for you?" Her heart rate kicked up a few beats. Had someone else been killed overnight? Was there another lead?

She heard footsteps on the other end of the line, then a door closing. Naomi's voice was so low Shelby almost couldn't hear her. "Someone filed a report last night."

Shelby frowned. "A report? What are you talking about?"

"A report on the Whitney Chandler investigation."

A sense of dread landed in her stomach like a bowling ball. Now her heart was racing. "Who filed it?" She suspected the answer, but a tiny part of her still hoped she was wrong.

A beat. "Detective Erickson."

Shelby hit mute and swore a blue streak. She returned to the call. "When? What does it say?"

"I sent a copy to your mail. It should be in your inbox. But the gist of it is that Bobby Garza killed Whitney, and we should bring him in ASAP. Detective Erickson mentioned Daniel Mendez, but then dismissed him for no motive."

"We don't know that." Shelby's voice rang inside her car.

Naomi audibly swallowed. "Yes, ma'am. I think he's trying to appease the captain, and maybe Whitney's parents. Make it look like we're progressing and close to an arrest."

"Close to an arrest? We don't even know where Bobby is." She realized she was shouting at Naomi. "Sorry. I don't mean to snap at you, Naomi. I'm just... upset."

"I know, ma'am." Naomi sighed. "I called because I didn't want you to be caught off guard when you came in this morning."

"I appreciate it. Really, I do. I'm off to pick him up now."

"Oh. That'll be fun."

"No kidding. Thank you, Naomi."

After she ended the call, Shelby inhaled through her nose and exhaled through her mouth. She focused on the seed head of a tall, dead blade of grass at the edge of the parking lot, emptying her mind. After Shawn died, her therapist had taught her this method of meditation: pick a small point in your line of vision, not too close, not too far away, then focus on it and your breathing. If a thought popped up, acknowledge it, then dismiss it. She did her best to focus on that golden seed head, watching it twitch in the frigid morning air. But the panic rising in her chest refused to be ignored, and thoughts of cutting Erickson from the investigation kept clouding her mind.

Finally, she gave it up for a poor job and reversed her car, coffee forgotten. Erickson's house wasn't far. Well, nothing was far from anything in Locust Grove. She used the short time in the car to prepare for any answers Erickson would give her when she asked him, "What the hell?"

Shelby banged on Erickson's front door. Behind her, the sun peeked through the sluggish clouds. She saw her face, pinched and angry, in the storm door's reflection. She waited, blood pounding in her ears, but didn't get a response.

The cool air was refreshing on her heated cheeks. She needed to have this out with Erickson now, before they drove back to the station. She was tempted to do something stupid, like file a formal complaint against him. Or punch him in the face. Neither of those were good options if she wanted to save face at the station.

A whiff of wood smoke caught her attention. She glanced at the chimney but didn't see any smoke. She sniffed, definitely scenting wood smoke. Her ears picked up a crackle of fire. She took off around the edge of the farmhouse and, sure enough, the scent and the sounds of a wood fire grew stronger.

Erickson stood next to his firepit, staring into the flames. The embers in the fire told Shelby he was burning yard debris. He was ready to leave, wearing his jacket, his arms crossed, eyes on the fire. His jaw was clenched. He must have known she'd come in guns blazing. "Hey, there, Reed."

She halted on the opposite side of the fire. The fire's heat warmed her front, leaving the rest of her chilly as her demeanor. "Tell me why I shouldn't request having you removed from this case."

He scratched the stubble on his cheek, eyes still fixed on the flames. "Because I did nothing wrong." His jaw ticked.

She blinked, then gave a low chuckle. "You don't think?"

He finally raised his eyes to hers. "No, I don't. And Guerrero doesn't think so, either."

She felt like he'd slapped her in the face. "You went to the captain with this before talking to me?"

He shrugged. "I knew what you'd say."

"Damn straight. And I'm right. Why did Guerrero accept your report? She knows what's at stake." Her heart slammed against her ribs. She felt her fingernails dig into her palms as her hands curled into tight fists.

Erickson cocked his head to the side and slipped his hands into the pockets of his jeans. "Do I?" He squinted at her.

"What do you mean? Of course, you do. We're trying to find—"

"We're trying to find a killer," he finished for her. "Why wouldn't we run down every possible lead, especially the one that makes the most sense?" He ran a hand through his hair. "How many times are we going to go over this? The forensic evidence points to Bobby. The kid has a flimsy alibi. He probably had a motive and we just need to drag him into the station and find out what it was. He's the killer. Everyone sees it except you."

He had a point, but he didn't understand. He hadn't had first row seats to his entire world crashing down. She swallowed. "I never said Bobby's not our man. I just need to make sure—"

He threw his hands in the air. "Make sure of what? He was her boyfriend. He has a history of violence. He has the jersey. He took off, disappeared. The only way he could look guiltier is if he showed up at the station with Whitney's phone and blood on his hands!" His voice rang through his backyard. The bird at the feeder took flight.

She crossed her arms over her chest, shifting her feet. The tension in her shoulders felt tighter than a bowstring. A log fell into the fire, popping. She watched it burn brighter and brighter, falling apart. She felt like that log.

How to make him understand? If she told him the entire story, how would he see her? Would he respect her or pity her? Would he still treat her like a partner? Probably not. He'd see her as weak. It had happened before, with other male partners. Being pushed behind a man, out of harm's way. Being left behind, even though running into danger was her damn job.

She cleared her throat. "He has an alibi."

He shook his head. "A thin one." He rested his hands on his hips. "Even the principal hinted that Bobby is the most likely suspect."

She scrunched her face. "He's not a detective. Wheeler is an ex-football player and private school administrator. He's only got gossip and hearsay. Speaking of which," she raised an eyebrow, "did you know Tom Long is on probation? For drinking and messing around with another teacher on school property?"

He rolled his eyes. "Tom Long is a non-starter. He's a mess, I'll give you that. But he's not our killer."

Shelby nearly snarled. "You've seen the videos. He clearly had some kind of obsession with Whitney."

He shook his head. "He was obviously enamored of her, but I think he'd be more interested in keeping her around, not killing her. And his alibi is stronger than Bobby's."

"What about Daniel Mendez? We haven't even talked to him."

He rolled his lips. "That's true. And we will talk to him. But Bobby's still our top suspect. He's in the wind, for Christ's sake. Why else would he run?"

"He's a kid! He's scared." She was breathing like she was running a 5K. The icy air shredded her lungs.

"Bullshit. Everyone's scared and no one else ran. Look," he walked around the fire pit to stand in front of her. "When I walked into the station last night, Guerrero pulled me into her office, firing questions at me. The Chandlers are turning up the heat and news outlets are circling like vultures." He rubbed his forehead. "I'm not used to this kind of pressure."

In the chilly morning, the fire lighting up his blonde hair, his breath coming out in clouds, Erickson suddenly looked vulnerable. "I thought the captain brought you in because you had experience. That you're the one who can handle the pressure with your—" she gestured up and down his front, "winks and your jokes."

"That's the idea. But," he threw his hands up and let them slap his thighs. "It's an illusion."

She blinked at him. Was this the same flirtatious, irreverent braggart who'd been drinking out of her mug that first day? "Explain."

He picked up a long stick from the grass and prodded the fire. Sparks flew up. The pile of logs and debris were almost gone. "You'll find this hard to believe." His voice took on a bitter edge. "But people tend to give me a lot of credit just because I'm—"

"A man?" Her eyebrows lifted while her lips pressed into a tight line.

"Yes." He held his arms wide, stick and all, like a showman on the stage. "But also, because I played football for a beloved team, and because, well." He fiddled with the collar of his jacket. "I'm good-looking."

Shelby let her eyes roll.

He hurried to say, "I've been told."

She chuckled, shaking her head. "Am I supposed to feel sorry for you?" She wanted to ditch him, but she could see there was something he needed to say.

"No, no, no. That's not what I mean." He broke the stick in two over his knee and tossed the pieces in the fire. "I mean, I feel like a fraud." He watched the stick burn in the fire pit.

She studied him, tilting her head. Of course, he'd had it easier as an officer and a detective than she did. She'd assumed that from the get-go. Most men did. But they usually relished their undeserved advantage if they weren't completely oblivious to it. Erickson, however, was ready to shed his armor of bias and face the enemy's slings and arrows without it. To wade into the weeds, get dirty. "Do you have a high success rate with closing cases?"

His eyes were wary. "Yes."

"Did you do the footwork on those cases?"

He rocked his head back and forth. "Mostly." He sighed. "But sometimes everyone gave me way too much credit. And I would try to explain, to give credit where credit was due, but nobody cared. Everyone was glad to move on, to close a case."

She nodded. "It doesn't sound like you're a fraud."

"But I feel like a fraud." His head fell back as he watched the clouds. "None of those cases were as high stakes as this one." He brought his attention back to her, counting off on his fingers. "Burglaries. Assault.

One homicide that was so easy to solve the killer might as well have turned himself in. This is different." He straightened to his full height, arms at his side, deadly serious. "I need a win. I need this."

She studied him, then said, "I understand." And she did. Every detective felt that drive to bring order to chaos, to right the wrongs. But anger flared in her ribs again. "But giving everyone, including the Chandlers, false hope, won't get us there. It will only make everything ten times more difficult." She stepped closer, nearly spitting in his face. "You have to play your cards close to the vest, keep your options open, until you're sure, so sure, you have your man. Then, and only then, do you go after him." She paced away. "If you give people false hope, then every move you make that doesn't point in the right direction is going to bring ten questions with it." She paced near the fire. "Everyone, especially the media, will ask why aren't we holding him? Why are we questioning someone else? Why do we need any other evidence? And then," she came back to him, toe to toe. "When it blows up in your face, and someone else gets killed, you'll wonder what the hell you'd been thinking. And you'll go to sleep every night seeing the face of not just one victim, but two." Her breath fogged the tight space between them. "That's not a win, Erickson."

Quietly, he asked, "Is that what happened to you?"

She swallowed. In her memories, she heard a gunshot, saw a river of blood, felt her world crumble in her hands. She stepped back. "Something like that."

The two detectives watched the last of the orange embers flicker out, leaving behind white ash that drifted into the breeze. A bird flitted to the feeder in the quiet.

"I thought filing a report would give us more time. Get Guerrero and the Chandlers off our backs." Erickson toed the edge of the fire pit.

"It probably did the exact opposite. It sped up the clock." Shelby bent to catch his gaze. His defenses were gone. He looked lost. "We will get the win. I promise."

He nodded. "Now what?"

She shrugged. "Now we work the case. Just like we have been." Erickson opened his mouth, but she said, "And if we have to drive around Locust Grove ourselves, we'll find Bobby Garza."

That earned her a small smile. Erickson bumped her foot with his. "Thanks."

Shelby searched the ground for a moment, then found what she was looking for. She picked up the bucket of sand and threw a few handfuls onto the few red cinders left in the pit, extinguishing them. Then she blew out a big breath and said, "My coffee's probably cold by now. Should we hit up Dunkin' on the way in?"

That earned her a huge smile. "Reed, you're singing my song."

Eighteen

Shelby and Erickson leaned against the hood of Shelby's Rav 4. They'd stopped at Sheetz instead of Dunkin' Donuts so Erickson could have apple cider donuts and pumpkin spice coffee. Erickson had scared her half to death because he'd squealed like a tween when he saw the Sheetz sign advertising the fall treats. Shelby sipped black coffee and munched on grapes, while Erickson chugged his flavored coffee and devoured his donut. She wondered what his yearly blood test results were like.

"We need to fill in some of these holes in Whitney's timeline," Shelby said. "When she left the party, who was still there? Did she see anyone on the way to the pool? Did someone give her a ride?"

Erickson swiped his forearm over his mouth. "True. But so far we have bupkis. We can only fill in the biggest hole in the timeline when we know who she met at the pool. And if we knew that," he tilted his head to meet her eyes. "We'd know who killed her."

"Probably."

"Probably?" He took a swig of coffee. "You think she could have met with someone and then a different person came along and killed her?"

"Or she met with two someones." Shelby watched a family rake leaves across the street. The parents raked gold leaves into piles, then the kids, their jackets flapping behind their little bodies, kicked through them, scattering their parents' hard work. The parents didn't seem to mind. "Although forensics didn't show that." She tossed her empty cup into the trash can. "I'm spiraling."

Erickson licked his lips. "I get it. Happens to me every year during my fantasy football draft." She glared at him. "Anyway, that pool was full of damp leaves and muck. Maybe there was more than one person, but the gunk and puddles destroyed the evidence."

"No. Forensics would have known if more than one person was there with Whitney."

He nodded. "Okay. Let's stick with the theory that she met with only one person until we see or hear anything that leads us to believe otherwise. That will make it easier to narrow down our suspects and follow the trail."

"Agreed." Across the street, the children shrieked as their parents threw piles of leaves at them. "So, we're solid on her timeline until she leaves that party."

Erickson swallowed. "Bobby, Del, and Skye all agreed on the time-frame."

Shelby crossed her feet at the ankles. "We haven't canvassed the houses along the probable route she would have taken to get to the pool."

Erickson turned to her, his eyebrows pulled together. "Everyone would have been asleep. Allegedly."

"But if they have security cameras or smart doorbells or even—"

"Have you seen those bird feeders with cameras?" His entire face lit up. "They work like Ring doorbells. The bird shows up, the camera starts recording, and sends the video to an app on your phone." He shakes his head in amazement. "Freakin' awesome."

Shelby waited a beat. "Then we should add bird feeders to the canvassing list, too." She retrieved her notebook and pen from her pocket. "I'll assign Will to it."

Erickson squinted, chewing his donut. "Maybe Boomers are right."

The non sequitur confused Shelby. "What are you talking about?"

"Big Brother. Pretty soon there'll be cameras everywhere. We're being watched all the time." He hunched his shoulders and wiggled his fingers.

She chuckled. "If only. Sure would make our jobs easier."

He held up a finger. "But at what cost?"

"One I'm willing to pay." She rested her hands on the hood behind her. "Back to Whitney. Bobby allegedly goes to bed. So does Del. Skye's at home. We need to talk to Daniel, and somehow we need to confirm Bobby's alibi beyond Del."

"The Chandlers were tucked up in bed, as well." Erickson picked up her thread. "Principal Wheeler and Tom Long didn't leave the conference until Saturday morning."

Across the street, the parents had stopped playing and shoveled their leaf piles into tall paper bags while their kids chased squirrels from tree to tree.

Shelby said, "Someone strong with large hands strangled Whitney."

"So, Skye's out, even if her alibi was shaky."

Shelby nodded. "Then there's the jersey." She narrowed her eyes at Erickson. "Wonder if Daniel Mendez has a red and white jersey?"

Erickson swiveled toward the trash can, aimed, and pitched his balled-up wrapper into it. Then his cup. He turned to Shelby, looking for praise. He reminded her of the kids across the street. When she remained quiet, he shrugged and dusted his hands. "He probably does. Everyone else at Bellmoor Prep seems to have one."

Shelby walked to the driver's side door. "Let's try Daniel Mendez at home. We're spinning our wheels until we talk to him or find Bobby." Once Erickson buckled his seatbelt, she said, "Do we know if Whitney was friends with anyone else on the Quiz Bowl team?"

"Not so far." He put on his sunglasses. The autumn sun blazed in the cloudless sky. "I dated a girl in high school who was on the Quiz Bowl team." Shelby said nothing, pulling out onto the street. "I used to run flashcards with her. Although, I don't think we ever made it through the whole stack, if you know what I mean." He looked at her sideways as his eyebrows bounced.

She shook her head. "Unfortunately, I do."

Daniel Mendez lived in a crowded, rundown trailer park that sat at the bottom of a hollow, along a wide, fast-flowing creek. Rust marks around the bottom borders of the trailers showed the high mark of the various times the creek had flooded. The Mendez's trailer sat in the back row of the park, crumbling in places, surrounded by discarded furniture, car parts, and grubby plastic toys. The dank, earthy smell of the creek met the detectives when they climbed out of Shelby's Toyota.

"No cars in the driveway." Erickson pointed his finger along the two dirt tracks that led to a ramshackle car port that sheltered more filthy furniture, old tools, and a broken sink. "Think anyone's home?"

Shelby climbed the steps to the front door, careful not to step on the trash that had accumulated there. She banged on the storm door. "Hello? Anybody home?" She waited a beat and banged again. Just as she was about to turn away, they heard a door open and close somewhere inside. She walked down a step, allowing the front door to swing open. Erickson stood behind her.

A thin woman pushed through the storm door. She had long stringy hair that had been dyed blonde some time ago, but now showed dark for several inches at the roots. She wore an oversized Aerosmith t-shirt that was torn along the hem and faded black leggings. "If you're looking for Damien, he ain't here." Her words slurred a little. She started back inside.

"Are you Mrs. Mendez? Daniel's mother?" Shelby reached out her hand, but didn't touch the woman.

The woman's eyes grew sharp. "Yeah. Who are you?"

"We're Detectives Reed," she pointed to herself, "and Erickson."

Mrs. Mendez raised her chin, crossing her bony arms. "What you want? What's Danny done now?"

Shelby gave Mrs. Mendez a small smile. "Nothing that we know of. His friend is," she paused, only for a split second, "missing. We'd like to talk to him, see if he can help us find his friend."

Mrs. Mendez was still wary. Clearly, she'd had dealings with law enforcement before. "Which friend?"

Erickson said, "Whitney Chandler."

Mrs. Mendez scrunched up her face. "He don't know any Whitney." Then she laughed, so loud it startled Shelby. "Sounds fancy. Trust me. He don't know anyone fancy."

Erickson rested an arm on the rusty, white railing, casual as could be. "Aw, you know how kids are. They don't tell their parents every-thing." He winked at her.

Shelby would have scoffed, but Mrs. Mendez giggled, actually gig-gled. "You're right about that. You know what?" She popped her hip, resting her fist on it. She leaned around Whitney to address Erickson. "Maybe he does know some girl named Whitney. You want to come in? Have a drink?"

"You've got to be kidding me," Shelby muttered into her shoulder.

Erickson beamed. "That's a tempting offer, but we can't drink on the job." Mrs. Mendez waved his protest away, but he continued. "Gotta be a good boy." She giggled again.

Shelby's grapes threatened to make a reappearance. She took her business card from inside her jacket and held it out to Mrs. Mendez. "If you see Daniel, would you have him call us? He's not in any trou-ble," Shelby reiterated. "We just need his help."

Mrs. Mendez took the card, but kept her eyes on Erickson. "And what if I just want to call?" She tried to slip the card in her bra, but missed her shirt. To cover her fumble, she held it to her chest.

Shelby opened her mouth, but Erickson said, "Now, Mrs. Mendez, what will dispatch think if you're calling me at all hours?" Another giggle, then gave a flirty wave and disappeared into the trailer.

Shelby turned and walked past Erickson toward the car, biting her tongue. Then she heard Mrs. Mendez say, "Wait, wait." Shelby turned around. Erickson, on her heels, did the same. Mrs. Mendez took one wobbly step down, leaning on the rickety railing. "I just remembered. He hangs out at the old Kmart sometimes. You might find him there tonight." She smiled, showing two gaps in her teeth. "I can show where it is, if you pick me up later."

Shelby showed her own teeth, not quite smiling. "We got it. Thanks." She got in the car and started it before she had to stomach any more of Mrs. Mendez's performance.

Nineteen

"I'm just saying," Erickson followed Shelby into the bullpen at the police station, "good looks aren't always a blessing." He shot her finger guns. "Sometimes they're a curse."

Shelby shrugged off her coat and slung it over her arm, perhaps with more force than necessary. Her jacket whacked Erickson in the face. "Oh, sorry." She hung it over the back of her desk chair while he mumbled something and smoothed his hair.

Will looked up from his desk. "What's up?"

Erickson leaned his hip on Will's desk. "Detective Reed is a little huffy because she couldn't get Mrs. Mendez to talk, but the ol' pearly whites," he pointed his thumbs at himself while he gave Will an enormous smile, "got her to meow like a kitten."

Naomi peeked out from behind her computer monitor. "Isn't the phrase 'sing like a canary?'"

Shelby thought of Mrs. Mendez draping herself over the trailer's railing. "Unfortunately, his description is apt."

Erickson nodded emphatically.

Shelby plopped into her swivel chair. "Officer Simon." Will gave her his attention. "It's possible a home camera caught Whitney leaving Bobby's and going to the pool. Map out the most likely route, then canvass those homes. See if anyone has a Ring camera or," she reluctantly nodded toward Erickson, who looked like he'd earned a gold star, "one of those video bird feeders. If they do, get the footage and see if you can spot Whitney and anyone who might have accompanied her."

"Got it." Will finished making a note. "We got my meemaw one of those bird feeders last Christmas. You'd think she was searching for the Zodiac Killer the way she keeps tabs on the comings and goings of those birds."

"Thank you." Shelby turned her chair toward Naomi. "Officer Kim, any word on Whitney's phone records?"

Naomi sat bolt upright. "Yes." She moved neat stacks of paper around until she pulled out a manila folder and flipped it open. "We have them."

"Wow." Erickson raised his eyebrows. "I thought her parents would be more of a problem, with the lawsuit and all."

Naomi said, "The captain spoke to them personally. She explained that if they wanted enough evidence to put Whitney's killer away for life, they should cooperate as much as possible with us, lawsuit and all." She smirked.

Shelby said, "What did you find?"

Naomi stood and walked to Shelby's desk, where she lay the file in front of her. "Nothing out of the ordinary in her recent calls or contacts. Her parents, Bobby, Del, Skye, Bellmoor Prep's office, and the occasional restaurant or shop." She pointed to a specific phone number. "And a few brief calls with Tom Long, including one the night she died."

Shelby eyed the date and time under Naomi's finger. "Maybe they talked about meeting up."

"Or, maybe," Erickson stepped behind Shelby to look at the file, "they talked about Quiz Bowl."

"Either way, we'll have to talk to him again." She asked Naomi, "Did his background check reveal anything?"

Naomi shook her head. "No. And I had his yearly evaluations pulled from Bellmoor Prep."

"Really?" Shelby leaned back in her chair, giving Naomi a small smile. "I'm impressed." Naomi smiled in return. "Anything?"

"He's on probation for drinking and," Naomi glanced at Erickson, "public display of affection on school grounds." She and Erickson shared a quiet giggle. Shelby bit the inside of her cheek.

"We heard about that." Erickson straightened and pulled up an empty chair. "A Miss Pugh?"

Naomi nodded.

"Officer Simon, did forensics find anything interesting in Whitney's locker?"

Naomi threw Erickson a shy smile, which he returned with a polite one, before returning to her desk. Will took her place, giving Shelby another file.

"Again, nothing out of the ordinary. Mirror, pictures of her friends, pictures of her and Bobby, her school stuff."

Shelby asked, "Did you read through her notes?"

"Yes." Will slumped dramatically, as if he'd run a marathon. "Teenage girls are so extra."

Shelby raised her eyebrows and waited. "Extra what?"

Erickson leaned back in his chair, clasping his hands behind his head, and giving Will a gun show Shelby would have preferred not to witness. "No, no. It's slang. 'Extra' just means over-the-top or exaggerated." He looked at Will for confirmation.

Will nodded like a bobble head. "Yeah."

"What made her so, uh, extra?" Shelby said.

"All the doodles. So many doodles." He waved his hands around as if he were drawing all over the station. "Stars, hearts, cats, dogs, balloons, bubble words." He crossed his arms. "Nothing useful. No suspicious names. No notes about dates or hook-ups."

"We know she was smart," Erickson said. "Too smart to put anything incriminating in her school stuff in case it got searched."

Shelby rubbed a finger back and forth over her lips. "Anything in coat pockets? Sweaters? Pencil bag?" She dropped her arm onto her armrest. "Anything? I'm desperate."

Will made a sympathetic noise. "She had three dried-up mums in her locker. Does that help?"

"What?" Shelby's eyebrows came together. "Was she in a gardening club?"

Will chuckled. "No. It's a tradition during football season, before homecoming."

"What is?"

"Lots of high schools do it as a fundraiser, usually for the booster club. Kids can buy a mum and have it delivered to someone during class. They have typed messages attached to the stem, like 'you're the *mum* that I want' or 'you're *mum* in a million.' Things like that."

Erickson wrinkled his nose like he'd drunk sour milk. "'You're the *mum* that I want?' Sounds like someone has a MILF fetish."

Shelby held up her hand to stop Erickson before he went on a tangent. Talking to Will, she said, "What did the messages say? And could you tell who sent them?"

He squinted at the ceiling. "There was one from Bobby," he hooked one forefinger over the other, "that said 'you're *mum* in a million.'"

"Thank God," Erickson said.

"There was one," he hooked the same forefinger over the first two fingers of the other hand, "from Del that said the same thing."

Shelby looked at Erickson. "Romantic, do you think?"

Erickson shrugged. "He said they're just friends and, frankly, I can't see that kid pulling a quarterback sneak on Bobby."

"We'll set that aside for now. And that last flower?"

Will hooked his finger over the other hand's three fingers, then made a fist. "Now, the third flower had a message, but it was anonymous."

Erickson dragged his hand down his face. "Of course it was. Couldn't have a message that said 'Whitney, meet me at the pool at midnight' with a clear-as-day signature, and we could take the W?"

Shelby ignored him. "What was the message?"

Will's face turned impish, like he was sucking on the juiciest candy. "'*Mum's* the word.'"

Twenty

Shelby killed her headlights and pulled into a parking space in the cracked lot. The old Kmart had closed years ago. It sat far back from the main road, behind a row of fast-food restaurants, which meant the abandoned lot provided excellent cover from prying eyes.

"'*Mum's* the word.' That message could be from anyone." Erickson sipped the last of his soda and placed his empty cup in a cup holder.

"True." Shelby zipped her jacket. "Maybe Tom Long?"

Erickson rocked his head back and forth. "It looks bad for a teacher to send a flower to a student. Can't imagine the boosters would have kept that to themselves."

"Also true." She peered out her windshield. "All right. Let's go."

Young people leaned against the storefront or sat on upturned milk crates, smoking and drinking. A few battered cars dotted the parking lot. Most of the kids had probably walked or caught a ride. The detectives could make out their faces in the bright screens of the kids' phones.

"I don't see Bobby," Erickson said, surveying the group over the roof of the car next to them.

"He wouldn't be here with this crew." Shelby scanned the faces along the storefront.

"Maybe if he were hiding?"

"I don't think they'd put up with him. They wouldn't want to draw attention."

"Well," Erickson pocketed his phone and zipped his jacket. "If they don't want to draw attention, they're going to love seeing us."

Shelby nodded. "Some of them will run. The smart ones won't. I'm counting on Daniel Mendez being one of the smart ones."

Erickson cocked his head and frowned at her. "I think 'smart' is a relative term here."

Shelby threw him a grin, then stepped out of the shadow of her car. Erickson did the same. They sauntered up to the storefront, keeping their faces as neutral as possible. Shelby heard "Oh shit," and a handful of kids took off running. The detectives kept their eyes on the rest of the group as they heard two cars race away behind them.

Shelby held up her hands, palms facing the kids. "We're not here to cause trouble. We don't care what you're smoking or drinking. We just want to talk to Daniel Mendez." Her gaze caught on a boy tossing his cigarette to the ground and grinding it out with his foot. He was difficult to see clearly in the dark, but he looked a lot like the photo in the student directory. Buzzed light brown hair, pale face, sharp cheekbones, and narrow, dark eyes. He kept his mouth shut, just waited.

Erickson said, "It's about Whitney."

Several heads turned in the pale boy's direction. He shoved his hands in his army-green jacket and tipped his chin toward the others. They turned back to their conversations, but kept their eyes on the detectives.

He walked away from the group and met the detectives in the parking lot. Daniel was shorter than both of them, with a wiry build. He raised his chin and threw his shoulders back, ready for a fight. Shelby kept her hands in her pockets, while Erickson left his loose at his sides.

Shelby said, "Are you Daniel Mendez?"

His dark eyes darted between theirs. "Yeah."

"I'm Detective Shelby Reed, and this," she tilted her head, "is Detective Jasper Erickson."

Daniel snorted. "Jasper? Seriously?"

Erickson smiled, baring his teeth. "Since the day my mama named me."

Shelby watched the two males size each other up. She said, "We want to ask you a few questions about Whitney Chandler."

Daniel shifted his attention to Shelby. "What about her?"

"When was the last time you saw her?" Shelby asked.

He sucked on his teeth, then said, "Friday, at school."

"When? Like, passing her in the hall?" Erickson asked.

"No, man," he chuckled, like Erickson missed a punchline. "Do I look like I'd take the same classes as Whitney?" When neither detective said anything, Daniel continued, "Nah, I saw her at lunch. She tutors me." He looked down, scuffing his shoes on the broken asphalt.

"You ever see her outside of school?" Shelby brought out her notebook and pen.

He shrugged. "Whitney and I don't exactly hang out with the same people, you know?"

"That's not what I asked."

He sucked his teeth again and looked back at the kids on the sidewalk. They were talking to each other, but occasionally glanced in Daniel's direction. He leaned toward Shelby and said quietly, "Sometimes."

"Sometimes what?" Shelby narrowed her eyes.

He shrugged again. "Sometimes I see her outside of school, like you said."

Erickson crossed his arms. "Did you ever meet at the pool?"

Daniel reared back, then shook his head, laughing. "No, man. The pool? Why the hell would we ever go there?" He kept shaking his head.

"Okay, then," Erickson said, "where?"

Daniel shifted from one foot to the other, his eyes scanning the parking lot.

Shelby said, "We don't care where. We just need to know." She studied him. "Was it somewhere off-limits at school?"

His eyes met hers. "Yeah. The theater. Backstage. In the dressing rooms, like."

"The theater?" Erickson snickered. Shelby cleared her throat, warning him. Daniel was already defensive. They didn't need to alienate him further.

"That's what I said." Daniel bit out the words.

She asked, "Isn't it locked? Did one of you have a key?"

He laughed again like the detectives weren't in on a joke. "You don't need a key. That door never locks right." With his hands in his pockets, he spread his jacket wide in a casual gesture. Shelby noticed he was wearing a faded red Bobcats jersey. Daniel said, "Everybody uses it for hookups or whatever."

Erickson said, "Were you hooking up with Whitney?"

"Yeah." Daniel tipped his chin up, puffing out his chest. "What? You think a girl like Whitney doesn't want me? Think again." Then he took two quick steps back. "Hey, this is between us, right?" He glanced over his shoulder at his friends. "You ain't gonna say anythin' to them, right?" He tipped his head backwards, toward the other teens.

"No." Shelby shook her head. "It's just between us."

"Why?" Erickson asked. "You worried Bobby Garza will find out?"

Daniel blew his lips like a horse and shook his head. "I ain't worried about Bobby. He knew all about me and Whitney."

"What?" Shelby's eyes popped.

"Yeah. She told him all about us. Said he didn't care, long as we kept it quiet. She said they both had reps to protect." He laughed. "I ain't got no rep. Well, a bad one. So, I didn't care. I was happy with the arrangement, you could say." He winked at Erickson, who remained stone-faced.

Shelby said, "You're sure Bobby knew? He wasn't jealous?"

"Nah, like I said. They're just for show. Me and Whitney are the real thing."

When they had interviewed Bobby, he'd seemed genuinely distraught. Shelby couldn't understand why Bobby wouldn't be jealous. But in today's world of polyamory and throuples, who knew? Of course, Daniel could be lying.

"She ever sell you drugs?" Erickson said. Daniel shuffled his feet. "Again, we don't care if she did. We just need answers so we can connect some dots."

"She used to."

Erickson shared a look with Shelby, then said, "Used to? You stopped using, or she stopped selling?"

Daniel shook his head. "Uh-uh. She stopped making me pay." He kept his eyes on the asphalt. "She said since we were a thing, she felt bad making me pay."

The lines bracketing Erickson's mouth deepened. "So, you traded sex for drugs?"

Daniel's head came up, and he pointed his finger in Erickson's face. Erickson didn't even flinch. "It isn't like that, alright? We have feelings for each other."

Erickson said, "I can't help noticing you keep using the present tense."

Shelby touched Erickson's arm and turned to the young man, who was clearly in love with Whitney. She didn't want to spook him until they'd asked him everything they wanted to know. "Daniel, you're wearing a Bobcats jersey. Were you wearing it Friday night?"

Daniel had trouble moving his eyes away from Erickson's to Shelby's. Eventually, he said, "Yeah. Wore it for the game."

"Where did you go after the game?"

"Here." He gestured with his pockets again. "I always hang with these guys here." He squinted. "None of us want to go home, you know what I mean?"

"Do they go to Bellmoor Prep with you?" Erickson asked.

"Couple of 'em."

"It's an expensive school. Do your parents pay for it? Or do you have a job?"

Daniel raised his chin. "I gotta scholarship. That's how come Whitney's been tutoring me, to help me stay there."

Shelby considered the boy. "Daniel, do you know why we're asking you all these questions about Whitney?"

"Is she in trouble?" His eyes widened. "Look, I know she was selling, but it wasn't anything bad, like. It's just Adderall and shit like that. She had to. She's saving up for college." He was working up a head of steam. "She's so smart, you know? And her parents can't afford to send her somewhere fancy like Harvard or whatever. So, she's saving up." He pointed his finger at Shelby. "She's got a plan with her supplier. She'll have enough to go. You watch."

Erickson lifted his eyebrows. "Supplier?"

Daniel nodded frantically. "Yeah. She's working up a plan with him to get a bigger cut. I mean, she does all the work, right? Why shouldn't she get a bigger cut?"

"Daniel," Shelby interrupted. "Do you know who her supplier is?"

"Hell, no." Daniel snorted. "I get in enough trouble. I don't need to get mixed up in all that." He sobered. "But Whitney's so smart. She knows how to play it."

"Daniel," Shelby said softly. "I'm afraid I have some bad news."

He must have seen something in her face because he suddenly looked like a wild animal, caught in a trap, eyes wide. "What?" He glanced between the detectives. "Wait, why are you asking all these questions about Whitney? Was she arrested?" He straightened and sniffed, ready for a fight again.

"No." Shelby felt pity for the lost, troubled young man. Whitney seemed to be the only light in his dark life. "She was murdered Friday night."

Daniel stared at Shelby for a moment, then spun on his heel and ran.

Twenty-One

"Shit," Erickson said.

He and Shelby sprinted after Daniel. The boy had a solid ten-yard lead on the detectives after catching them by surprise. But his smoking habit slowed him down enough that the fit detectives caught up to him quickly. When he reached a grassy berm, Erickson leaped into the air and wrapped his arms around Daniel's knees, bringing him down with a grunt. Daniel squirmed under Erickson, yelling, "Just let me go!" But Shelby stepped forward, chest heaving, and handcuffed Daniel's hands behind his back.

Erickson stood and pulled Daniel up with him. Daniel pressed his lips against the sobs that were fighting to break free. Tears streamed down his gaunt face. "Let me go," he hiccuped.

"Running's not a good look," Erickson panted. "Why did you run?"

A wounded moan escaped Daniel's lips. "I didn't do nothin'. Just let me go." He hung his head.

Shelby rested her hands on her hips, the freezing night air burning her lungs. "Sorry. If you won't stay and answer our questions, we're taking you in. While you're at the station, our officers can verify your alibi with the others."

While Erickson read Daniel his rights and lead him to Shelby's car, Shelby called for Naomi and Will to come to the parking lot and question the spooked teens. They'd have to sort through a lot of snark to get them to cooperate, but Naomi wasn't much older than the kids standing around smoking and drinking. Probably knew most of them. She could get them to talk.

As Shelby climbed into her car, dispatch repeated the BOLO for Bobby over the police radio.

From the back seat, between wet hiccups, Daniel said, "You lookin' for Bobby Garza?"

Shelby met his eyes in the rearview mirror. "Yes. Do you know where he is?"

Daniel smirked, wiping his nose on his shoulder. "I gotta pretty good guess."

Erickson turned his head toward Daniel, and with a mock-friendly smile, said, "Don't keep us in suspense."

"You check Del Coleman's house?"

Shelby frowned, her eyes still on Daniel. "We were there before, questioning him."

Daniel sniffed. "Bet you a hundred bucks he's hiding Bobby."

Shelby shared a look with Erickson. He raised his eyebrows as if to say, *it's worth checking out.*

The detectives left Daniel at the station. They would question him later. He seemed relieved when they locked him in a cell by himself. He sat on the bench, head in his hands. Shelby heard quiet sobs before she walked away.

Her phone buzzed in her pocket. She checked the screen.

Dad: Thanks for stopping by last night. Remember what I said. Be careful.

"Love you too, Dad." She pocketed her phone and kept moving.

In the bullpen, Erickson called in a favor with a local judge, pulling her away from a dinner party to sign a warrant to search the Coleman's house.

"Why does she owe you a favor?" Shelby asked.

"Her kid wanted to play football, but he was worried he'd get cut. Her husband deployed to Afghanistan during tryouts, so her son and

I worked together a few times. I taught him some basic drills and gave him a simple circuit training plan. He made the team. Starting line-up, too." He narrowed his eyes. "Were you thinking something salacious about the judge and me, Detective? For shame." He shook his head and made a clicking sound. Shelby ignored his jab and walked away.

In the car on the way to Del's, Erickson said, "Daniel's taking Whitney's death pretty hard."

Shelby nodded. "Harder than I would have expected."

"If he was as close to Whitney as it seems, maybe Bobby got jealous, regardless of what Daniel said."

"That's a definite possibility." Shelby glanced at Erickson. "Or Daniel lied about their relationship altogether, and he's actually upset he got caught."

Erickson shook his head. "His fingerprints are on the condom box. And I bet after Naomi and Will talk to those kids, he'll have a solid alibi." He waved his hand in her direction. "Here you are again, deflecting attention away from Bobby, the kid with the motive, strength," he pulled at his jacket with his thumbs and forefingers, "and a jersey that all say he killed Whitney." His eyes were bright, his face reflecting the glow of her dashboard lights.

Her nostrils flared. "Don't forget, he has an alibi, too."

He pointed a finger at her. "A thin one, at best. He was home all night? Del stayed to clean up? If Del is hiding Bobby, then he sure as shit lied about being with him the night Whitney was killed."

They rode the rest of the way in silence. A wisp of hope fluttered in Shelby's chest that Bobby would be at Del's, but she quickly snuffed it out. No sense putting the cart before the horse, as her mother used to say.

She rang the Colemans' doorbell. Del's father answered the door. He looked wary, and a little angry. "Detectives, what can I do for you?"

Shelby held up the warrant. "Mr. Coleman, we have a warrant to search your house. We received a tip that Bobby Garza may be hiding out here."

Color rose in Mr. Coleman's face. "First of all, you are way off base. You clearly don't know how to do your job, because Bobby Garza wouldn't touch a hair on that girl's head. Second, how dare you accuse me of hiding someone in my own house?"

Erickson said, "Sir, if you'll step aside? This won't take long."

Del appeared in the hallway behind Mr. Coleman. "Dad? What's going on?"

Mr. Coleman waved Del away, keeping his eyes on the detectives. "Nothing for you to worry about. The detectives think Bobby's hiding somewhere in our house."

Del froze, and the blood drained from his face. "He's not here."

Shelby held out the warrant to Mr. Coleman, who finally accepted it, but didn't bother to look at it. "We won't interrupt your evening any longer than we have to. The sooner you let us in, the sooner we can take care of this matter." She widened her stance. "Please don't make us use force."

Mr. Coleman's face grew red and splotchy. He snarled, but moved aside. As soon as Shelby stepped across the threshold, they heard a door slam on the opposite side of the house. Del's head whipped in that direction.

"Not again," Erickson growled, as he tore past Mr. Coleman and Del toward the back of the house.

Shelby spun on her heel and raced down the front sidewalk. When they'd visited the Colemans in the daytime, she'd noticed a high fence surrounded the backyard. Either Erickson would trap Bobby there, or—

She heard footsteps thudding on the ground, coming closer. She threw herself around the corner, slamming into Bobby Garza. He was much taller and heavier than she was, but her shoulder hit his solar plexus, and he fell to the ground, wheezing. Before he could get up, she pinned his arms with her knees and sat on his heaving chest.

Erickson burst through the backyard gate, pulling up when he spotted them. "Damn kid jumped the fence." He glanced over his shoulder at the wooden planks. "You're wasted on the D-line. You thought of playing wide receiver? Or tight end?" Erickson bent over, placing his hands on his knees to catch his breath.

Bobby didn't fight them. He closed his eyes, letting his body go limp.

Mr. Coleman and Del came up behind Shelby as she stood up. Del, his eyes wet and as big as hard-boiled eggs, watched Bobby cover his face with his hands. Del swallowed hard. "We have to tell them."

Bobby, his hands still blocking his face, shook his head.

"Yeah, we do." Del looked at his father. "It's time."

Twenty-Two

Atear crawled down Bobby Garza's ebony cheek. He wiped it away with the sleeve of his varsity jacket. His bloodshot eyes focused on his handcuffed wrists, chained to the table in front of him. Being on the run had taken its toll on him.

Shelby and Erickson sat on the opposite side of the table from Bobby in an interrogation room. A blinking red light on the video camera hanging from the ceiling was the only movement in the room. They gave Bobby a moment to collect himself.

Shelby placed her notebook on the table and clicked her pen. "Bobby, where were you Friday night after the party broke up? You told us you were home, but I don't think that's true." Although her voice was soft, her shoulders tightened like a winch, pulling and pulling. She sat up, trying to release the strain, trying to decide if she wanted Bobby to be guilty. If he was, her job would be easier and harder at the same time.

"Bobby," Erickson said, "you need to come clean. You ran. You hid. It doesn't look good. But if you tell us the truth, we can try to help you." He clasped his hands loosely on the table, but a muscle twitched in his jaw. "Where were you?"

Bobby swallowed and slumped deeper into his chair. "Where's Del?" He didn't look at the detectives. His voice was rough and low.

"He's next door," Shelby said. "Depending on what you tell us, we may charge him with harboring a fugitive and obstruction of justice." Del was still a minor, but a suspicion was growing in Shelby's mind, and she knew what buttons to push now.

Bobby's face crumpled. "Where's my mom?"

Shelby said, "She's out front, waiting on the lawyer she called."

Erickson ducked his head, trying to catch Bobby's eye. "Do you need a lawyer, Bobby?" He tilted his head. "Why did you kill Whitney?"

Bobby shook his head and finally met Erickson's gaze. "I didn't kill Whitney. And I don't care about a lawyer." Another tear snaked down his cheek. This time, he ignored it. "I'll tell you whatever you want to know. Just don't do anything to Del."

Erickson frowned, then looked at Shelby. She said, "Did Del kill Whitney?"

Miserable, Bobby swung his focus to Shelby. "You got it all wrong." He shook his head again, looking at a point over Shelby's shoulder. "We had it all planned. We were going to wait until after graduation, when we went to college. Then we'd be on our own."

Erickson's forehead wrinkled, and he blinked. "Who? You and Whitney? What did you plan?"

Bobby took a big breath. "No. Not me and Whitney. Me and Del. None of this would be happening if Whitney hadn't gone and gotten herself killed."

Erickson huffed. "Bobby, if you don't start telling us what happened—"

"I was with Del that night." Angry words burst out of Bobby. "After the party, I went home with Del. We stay at his place every Friday night, 'cause his mom works and his dad takes Ambien. He's always out cold, doesn't hear a thing. Then I go home before my parents wake up, and they think I've been home all night." His eyes blazed as they danced between the detectives.

The pieces clicked into place. Shelby said, "You and Del are—"

"Gay," Bobby said, jutting his chin, daring one of them to judge him. "He's my boyfriend." His eyes dropped to the table. "But no one knows."

Shelby remembered Daniel's snide comment about where Bobby had been hiding. Erickson must have, too, because he said, "I think a few kids know. Maybe more." Bobby's eyes widened.

Although they needed more information, Shelby was hopeful. Her gut told her that Bobby was finally telling the truth. That whatever happened with Whitney, he didn't kill her. The relief made her a little lightheaded. "Bobby, walk us through that night, starting after the football game."

"It's like I said before, a bunch of us went to my house for the after-party."

"Including Del and Whitney?" Erickson asked.

"Yeah, of course."

"Then what? What time did everyone leave?"

"The party started breaking up around eleven-thirty. Me, Del, and Whitney cleaned up." He looked at Shelby. "Whitney took off, then me and Del went to his place."

Shelby made notes. "Did Whitney say where she was going? If she was meeting someone?"

"Nah. I figured she was hooking up with Daniel."

"Daniel Mendez?" Erickson said. When Bobby nodded, he said, "What made you think that?"

"I knew she wasn't going home. She would have asked us to take her. And if she went out at night, and it wasn't with me, it was to hook up with Daniel."

"So, you knew about Whitney and Daniel," Shelby said, "but it didn't bother you?"

Bobby rolled his eyes. "Did you not hear me say I'm with Del?"

"Was this a poly kind of situation?" Erickson furrowed his brow and waved a hand in the air. "Were the three of you a throuple?"

Bobby glared at Erickson. "Hell, no. Look, I'm not out. I can't be. I'm banking on a football scholarship."

Shelby shrugged. "So? I thought kids today were okay with someone being gay."

"Kids, yeah. But name one NFL player who's out and proud." He raised his eyebrows.

"I know little about football."

"No one." Erickson leaned back in his chair. "No one in the NFL is out, let alone proud."

Shelby looked at Erickson. "What does that have to do with a college football scholarship?"

Erickson rested his elbows on the arms of his chair. "Trickle-down effect. The NFL scouts players from colleges. If no one who plays for the NFL admits to being gay, then no one on the college level will, either."

Shelby nodded. "And, consequently, no one who plays high school football, if they want to be recruited by a college."

Bobby nodded. "Now you get it."

"Then, why date Whitney? Why bother?" She crossed her arms on the table, leaning forward.

He swallowed. "A couple summers ago, Del and I were hanging out in the state park. We went off the trail to have some privacy, but a couple of Bellmoor Prep kids saw us."

"I'm guessing," Erickson said, "you weren't picking wildflowers."

Bobby glared at him, then continued. "The guy knew us from football, but he and his girlfriend had graduated. So, they didn't have time to spread any gossip about us before they went off to college."

"But you got scared," Shelby supplied.

Bobby nodded. "I was already friends with Whitney, so the three of us came up with a plan to keep me and Del a secret. Whitney didn't mind, because dating me made her more popular with the jocks at school."

"And it took the heat off her relationship with Daniel," Erickson added.

Bobby nodded again.

Shelby made some notes. "So, you and Whitney only dated as a smokescreen for your relationship with Del and her relationship with Daniel. And you were with Del all night Friday night?"

"Until about five a.m." Bobby said. "Then I went home." He dragged a large hand down his face. "Now everything is a bust. My parents will know. Del's parents. The entire school. Goodbye football scholarship."

"Not necessarily," Erickson said. He shared a brief smile. Now that Bobby wasn't their top suspect, Erickson seemed to soften toward the boy. "Times are changing. A handful of college players have come out. That football scholarship is still possible." He held his hands wide. "It's not like you need to put out a press release."

Bobby just shrugged, still looking defeated.

"Bobby," Shelby said, "we're trying to find out more about Whitney's drug supplier. Do you know who it was?"

He leaned back in his chair, waving his hands in front of him. "No. I didn't want any part of that. Whitney knew to keep all that to herself. I had my own secret to keep, you know?"

As Erickson unlocked Bobby's cuffs, he said, "Did anything happen in the last few months that caught your attention? Maybe it wasn't a big deal at the time, but now it seems suspicious."

Bobby said, "Wait. I kinda remember something." His eyebrows pulled together.

"About Whitney?" Shelby asked.

"Yeah." Bobby rubbed his wrists where the cuffs had been tight. "I remember this one time, she was supposed to meet me after practice, but she didn't show. I got worried and texted her. She didn't text back, but she was at my house when I got home. I told her it scared me when I didn't hear from her, and she said something like, 'That guy's not scary. He's a big teddy bear.' Then she laughed, and said, 'If only his kids knew what their dad was really like.'" Bobby looked at Shelby. "I didn't ask her anything else because, like I said, I didn't want to know. Is that something?"

Her stomach twisted like someone had their fist on her guts. "Yes, it is. Thank you."

After they'd released Bobby and Del, and sent them away with their parents, Erickson said, "I don't know a lot of teddy bears, but most of the dads that come through the station are pretty damn scary."

Shelby nodded, re-sketching the picture in her mind of Whitney's killer from a teenager to someone older. A father.

Erickson said, "Detective Reed? Welcome to square one."

Twenty-Three

The night pushed against the station's windows, a chill leaving lacy frost in the corners of the panes. The adrenaline that had been propelling Shelby through the long day finally drained away. At her desk, she rested her head against the back of her chair, her mind flatlining. The mental gymnastics required to adjust their perspective on Whitney's case wore her out.

She heard footsteps approach. "I'd say, 'You don't have to go home, but you can't stay here,' except you should go home and get some sleep." Erickson sat against the edge of her desk, fiddling with the sticky notes on her desk.

She lifted her head. "Same goes for you. Though, I don't know how much sleep I'll get, trying to figure this out. I have a feeling I'll be seeing a Rolodex of our adult male suspects flipping through my dreams all night."

He yawned as he said, "Does anyone even know what a Rolodex is anymore?"

She chuckled. "Probably not. Unless it's from a TikTok video." She took the sticky notes from him and set them on the other side of the desk.

"True." He picked up a pen and flipped it end over end. "It looks like we've ruled out Bobby." He watched her. "You must be relieved."

She took the pen and put it aside. "I'm glad we can scratch off a suspect from our list." The truth was, she was more relieved than she wanted to admit, even to herself. "As for Whitney's supplier, we can start with known dealers in the area. Start shaking trees and see who falls out." She stood, sliding her arms into her jacket and slinging her bag over her shoulder.

"Right." Erickson stood as well, shoving his hands into his pockets, swelling his impressive chest. Golden stubble covered his jaw, and his eyes drooped with fatigue. After spending so much time with him, she could acknowledge that he was a good detective, and that they worked well together once they found their rhythm. He said, "Although the local dealers I know are more in the meth and H business than they are Adderall and Ambien."

She nodded. "But it's the only place we have to start."

It was quiet in her car on the way to Erickson's house. In his driveway, she opened her mouth, closed it, then tried again. "Thank you for your help today."

He leaned back, raising his eyebrows. "Why, Detective Reed, control yourself. Such displays of emotion are uncalled for."

She glared at him, but pressed her lips against smiling. "Don't make me regret saying it."

He grinned, dimples appearing in his cheeks. She hadn't noticed them before. Of course, he would have dimples. Then, he climbed out of her car, whistling "Maneater." She smiled and shook her head. After he was safely inside, she headed for home.

Her house was completely dark. She'd neglected to leave on a light, not expecting to be gone so long. Her house was a small rancher, which suited her perfectly as a single woman with no children. She parked in the garage, then entered through the door that led into her kitchen. Before she could flip the light switch, a loud mewl broke the silence.

"Hello, to you, too, Queenie."

In the kitchen's light, her fluffy tabby cat paced in front of her, crying for her dinner. Shelby picked her up for a cuddle, but Queenie was having none of it. She squirmed out of her arms and stood with her front paws on a cabinet, looking upward, where she knew Shelby kept the cat food.

"All right, all right. I'm sorry I'm so late."

Shelby prepared Queenie's dinner, setting it on a vinyl mat decorated with rainbow colored paw prints. Queenie attacked the meaty morsels as if she hadn't eaten in weeks, not just mere hours.

Queenie satisfied, Shelby changed into a faded West Virginia University t-shirt and sleep shorts. As she brushed her teeth, she wondered who on earth Whitney's supplier was. He had to be someone local enough to meet Whitney at the deserted pool in the middle of the night. He also had to be working with doctors or pharmacists who kept him in business. And according to Whitney, he was a father. Tomorrow, Whitney would suggest to Erickson that they interview not only known street drug suppliers, but also pharmacists in the area, including the hospital's.

Shelby climbed into bed, absolute exhaustion already tugging on her consciousness. She heard paws padding down the hallway and into her room, then a mound of soft fur nearly smothered her. Soft purrs rumbled in the vicinity of her chest. "Okay, okay. Lie down. It's not playtime." She scratched Queenie's head and cheeks before the cat climbed over her to curl up at her back. Shelby knew she would wake up stiff in the morning, having remained stationary all night so as not to disturb Queenie. But the cat's solid warmth was a comfort, no matter the price.

A crash startled Shelby awake.

She sat bolt upright, listening. Queenie leaped off the bed with a disgruntled meow. In the deafening silence, Shelby leaned sideways and punched in the four-digit code on the gun safe that sat on her nightstand. She pulled her department issued Smith & Wesson from the safe, and loaded it with a full clip. She slid from her bed and braced herself against the bedroom wall, next to the door. Wind whistled through a distant room of the house and cold air wrapped itself around her like a constrictor. Shivering, she listened hard, but heard no footsteps, only the blood pounding in her ears. Readying her pistol, she swung into the hallway, flipping on the light switch.

Nothing.

An icy breeze caressed her skin as she crept down the hallway. When she reached the end, she took a breath, then spun into the living room. Pieces of glass sparkled on the carpet in the light from the streetlamp in front of the house. A hole about the size of a dinner plate gaped in the center of her bay window.

She cleared the rest of the house, flipping on every light as she went. The house was empty.

Shelby slipped on a pair of hard-soled gardening shoes that sat by the back door and returned to the living room. The thudding in her ears rivaled her heart's drumming in her chest. Tingles ran down her back and sent shock waves into her fingers. She placed her pistol on the coffee table and stared at the brick on the floor. It was wrapped in a piece of paper held in place with a length of twine.

She retrieved a pair of nitrile gloves from her work bag and yanked them onto her hands. Trembling with cold, anger, and adrenaline, she unwrapped the note from the brick. Three words in black marker stared at her from the page: BOBBY DID IT.

Twenty-Four

The next morning, Erickson strolled into the station an hour after Shelby. She'd had a restless night after duct taping a piece of cardboard she pulled from her recycling bin over the hole in her window. The whistling of the wind kept weaving through her dreams, inspiring scenes of her searching for Shawn in a deserted hospital. If she could just find him, she could save him. Her cheeks were wet every time she woke.

Queenie deserted her before the sun was up, tired of Shelby's tossing and turning. Shelby finally gave up at five a.m., showered, dressed, and drove to the station, taking the brick and the note with her in evidence bags.

She was staring at photos of their suspects taped to a whiteboard in the conference room when Erickson plunked an insulated tumbler in front of her. "Coffee. Just how you like it. And lots of it." He was carrying a plastic tumbler filled with what looked to be a protein shake. "Got your text about driving separately. I thought only farm hands got up that early. Did you eat?" She shook her head, frowning at him. "Want some of my shake? Lots of good stuff in here." He tipped it back and forth, then took a swig. A frothy mustache appeared on his upper lip before he licked it off.

"No, thank you. I'll get something later." She picked up the to-go cup. "Thank you for this." She hadn't even bothered to make herself a cup of coffee yet. Her mind was entirely consumed with the note and who might have thrown it through her front window.

Erickson dropped his bag on the conference room table and stood in front of the whiteboard, studying it. She said, "I had a break-in last night."

He spun to face her, eyes wide. "What? Shit. Are you okay?" He set down his shake and sat next to her. He reached out like he was about to pull her into a hug, but thought better of it. His arm fell to his side. "What happened?"

"I'm okay." She gave him a small smile. "Around one a.m., someone threw a brick through my front window." His brows knit together, and his jaw stiffened. "They tied a note to it. It said, 'Bobby did it.'" She lifted her eyebrows.

"'Bobby did it?'" Erickson said. He looked at the whiteboard, rubbing his jaw, then met her eyes. "Well, that's confusing."

She sighed. "I think it's the killer's clumsy attempt to put us back on to Bobby as a suspect." She took a sip of coffee. Hazelnut. It was flavorful and hot. She lifted her cup in thanks before setting it down. "After questioning him yesterday, my gut tells me he didn't kill Whitney, and he has nothing to do with whatever she was mixed up in."

He nodded. "I agree. That kid practically bled his heart out all over the table. He and Del are probably dealing with a whole different can of worms today." He grimaced.

"No doubt." She sipped again.

"Where's the note now?"

"I left with it with forensics, but no one's coming in for another..." she checked her watch, "hour." When he scoffed, she said, "Patience is a virtue."

He waved his hand in the air in a dismissive gesture. "It probably won't tell us anything, anyway."

"I don't think so, either." She leaned on her forearms on the table. "What it does tell us is that the killer somehow knows we moved on from Bobby." He narrowed his eyes. "As much as I'd like to think all our officers are as professional as they come, this is a small town. One word to someone's partner, mother, whomever, and news will spread. All it takes is a few texts."

Erickson studied the whiteboard. "Bobby's out. Del is out. Daniel has an alibi, but any of those kids might cover for him." He looked at Shelby. "But I don't think so."

"Me, either. After Officers Kim and Simon questioned them last night, they released Daniel. We didn't have enough to hold him once they vouched for him."

"Skye?" He squinted. "I know she doesn't have big hands, but maybe she put someone up to it?"

"Who? She's not dating anyone. Not only that, but what would her motive be? I don't see her killing Whitney just to take the valedictorian spot."

Erickson scrubbed his face with his hands. "This is ridiculous. We need new leads."

"We know her supplier was a father. Today we'll talk to the usual suspects in the area, see if anyone knows anything. And I asked Will to interview the local pharmacists. There aren't many."

"If they're willing to talk," Erickson said. "I think we should bring Daniel back in. Even if he didn't kill her, he has to know who else was buying from her."

"Think there was a lot of pillow talk in the theater's dressing room?" Shelby threw him a doubtful look.

Erickson barked out a laugh. "Who knows?" He tapped Shelby's shoulder lightly with his fist. "I like the lighter side of Detective Reed."

She playfully brushed off her shoulder. "Don't get used to it." She scooped up her bag and her coffee and stood. "The local dealers will still be in bed. Might as well pay them a visit while we can catch them at home."

Erickson rose and grabbed his tumbler. "Same with Daniel."

They drove to every rundown house, duplex, apartment building, and bolt hole for the dealers they'd tangled with. After the derelicts cursed, put on pants, and squinted at the detectives in the morning light, every one of them denied knowing anything about Whitney's business. Most of them didn't even know her name. Furthermore, most of them insisted they didn't deal in "kid stuff" like Adderall. The few who did said they sold to parents more often than kids, which Shelby and Erickson weren't happy to hear. At nine-thirty, they finished interviewing the last dealer. He slammed the door on them, and they climbed into Shelby's car.

Erickson dropped his head against the seat and closed his eyes. "That was a bust."

"We knew it would be." She shrugged. "But we had to check it off our list."

He rolled his head in her direction and opened his eyes. "Mind driving through Dunkin' Donuts on our way back to the station?"

"Really?" Shelby backed onto the street where traffic had picked up since they'd started their search.

"I'm hankering for hot chocolate and a glazed." He rubbed his palms along his thighs. "Plus, we can take some to the station. Earn more brownie points." He turned his Colgate smile on her.

She shook her head. "Shameless. They're colleagues. We shouldn't need brownie points." She threw him a teasing look. "Besides, I think your scorecard is overflowing with brownie points."

"Sure." He nodded, then tilted his head toward her again. "But you never know when you'll need to cash them in."

After they picked up a hot chocolate and glazed donut for Erickson, another coffee for Shelby, and two dozen assorted donuts for their fellow officers, they were welcomed at the station like heroes returning from war.

"Forensics examined the brick and the note you gave them," Naomi said around a mouthful of cinnamon sugar donut. "The report's in the conference room."

"Thank you, Officer Kim," Shelby said.

Before she could walk away, Naomi added, "And Principal Wheeler called."

"What did he want?"

"He said he's fielding a lot of calls from parents who are worried about sending their kids back to school tomorrow. They're worried their kid might be next, I guess."

Shelby stifled a sigh. She doubted they were dealing with a serial killer or anyone who was targeting kids at random. But she understood how a parent would be worried about their child's safety. "What did you tell him?"

Naomi's eyes widened. "I didn't tell him anything. I told him you'd call him."

Shelby pursed her lips. "Thank you for deferring to me, Officer Kim. In the future, I authorize you to tell him we are working as fast as we can, but we aren't obligated to keep him apprised of our investigation."

"Oh, right." She brushed a crumb from the corner of her mouth.

Shelby paused. Naomi knew just about everyone in Locust Grove. "Officer Kim, did you tell anyone that we released Bobby?" When Naomi choked on her donut, Shelby said quickly, "I'm not accusing you of anything. It may have been a harmless conversation with your mother, for instance."

Naomi's head shook back and forth fast enough to swing her smooth, black hair. "No, ma'am. I don't discuss any police business with civilians, no matter who they are or what they're offering."

"Offering?" Shelby's brow furrowed.

Naomi rolled her eyes. "There are a couple of gossip girls I went to school with who try to bribe me with designer stuff to give them the four-one-one. But they don't get squat out of me." She looked very proud.

Erickson joined them, leaving the officers around the donut box laughing at something he'd said. He winked at Shelby and threw a thumb over his shoulder. "Brownie points."

Shelby said, "Officer Kim just informed me that Principal Wheeler called to get an update on the case because he has a lot of worried parents calling him."

"Or maybe he wants an update for himself," Erickson said.

"Could be." Shelby frowned. "I wonder..."

Erickson crossed his arms, popping his biceps. "Wonder what?" Naomi was transfixed.

Shelby cleared her throat, and Naomi studied her monitor. "I wonder if the principal had any idea what Whitney was up to, and if he could point us toward her other clients."

"Wouldn't he have already said as much?"

"Not if he wanted to preserve the reputation of the school. How would it look if word got out that the valedictorian-to-be sold drugs at school?"

He nodded. "I see your point." He slipped into his jacket as Shelby retrieved the forensics report on the brick and the note from the conference room. "Stop number one, Daniel. Stop number two, Principal Wheeler." He tipped his chin toward the report she was reading. "What's the verdict?"

She pursed her lips. "Exactly what we thought." She looked at him and threw the report on her desk. "Absolutely no help whatsoever."

Twenty-Five

Daniel was already outside, smoking a cigarette on the front steps to the trailer where he lived, when the detectives arrived.

He scowled, not bothering to stand when they approached. "What do you want?" His eyes were red and puffy.

"We want to talk about Whitney a little more," Shelby said.

A thud came from inside the trailer, followed by a loud male voice. Both detectives lifted their heads toward the voice, eyes on the trailer, but Daniel waved a hand. "My old man's in a shit mood this morning. Don't pay any attention."

Shelby and Erickson shared a look.

Erickson said, "Is he in a shit mood a lot?"

Daniel flicked ash into the scrubby grass. "Like I said, what do you want?"

Shelby flipped through her notebook. "Did Whitney ever talk about Mr. Long?"

"The Quiz Bowl coach?" When Shelby nodded, Daniel said, "I mean, yeah. Sometimes."

"What did she say?"

One side of his mouth lifted. "What a loser he is. How he was always coming on to her."

Erickson rested his hands on his hips. "Coming on to her? In what way?"

Daniel waved his cigarette around. "Not like you're thinking. Like, kissing up to her because he knew she was Wheeler's favorite." He leaned forward, elbows on knees. "I don't know if you've heard, but he was about to get shit-canned."

Erickson nodded. "We heard something about that."

"Yeah, so he was always kissing up to Whitney, getting her to do TikToks with him, for Christ's sake." He laughed, then his face fell, as if he had forgotten for a minute that Whitney was dead, then remembered.

"Did she meet with him very often?"

His eyes wet, Daniel said, "Hell, no. They did Quiz Bowl shit, but if she had any free time, she spent it with me."

Shelby said, "When you and Whitney met in the theater dressing room, did she ever talk about her business? Other clients? Or her supplier?"

Daniel took a drag from his cigarette, breathing out smoke from his nose. In the chilly morning air, the clouds billowed even larger. "She mentioned some of the other kids she gave shit to."

"Like who?"

He squinted at Shelby as he took another drag. "Who's to say?"

Shelby tilted her head. "We're not interested in arresting anyone for possession. We're just chasing answers, looking for anyone who could fill us in on the questions we have about who killed Whitney."

He dropped his head and rubbed his thumb between his eyebrows.

When he was quiet for almost a minute, Erickson said, "Okay, you don't want to rat out any kids. What about adults? We think whoever supplied Whitney was an adult male with children. Did she ever talk about him?"

A crash from inside the trailer interrupted Daniel. The noise sounded like someone throwing pots and pans around the kitchen.

The same male voice bellowed something they couldn't understand. A screechy female voice answered it from the other end of the trailer.

Daniel raised his eyes to the sky. "I told you, I didn't want any part of what she was doing. I didn't let her talk about it." He rubbed his chest absentmindedly with his free hand.

"Anything she said, no matter how small, would help us." Erickson rested his foot on the bottom step. "Look, man, I'll level with you. We're stuck. We're running out of leads and out of time. For all we know, this guy will kill again. Maybe you're next, just for hanging out with Whitney."

Shelby crossed her arms and threw Erickson a sharp look.

But what he said got Daniel's attention. "Me? I'm next?" He looked around, as if the killer were lurking behind the carport.

Erickson shrugged. "Who's to say?" He gave Daniel a tight smile. "Until we put this guy behind bars, we don't know who's safe and who's not."

With wide eyes, Daniel nodded fervently. "Lemme think." His forehead scrunched. Then he looked at the detectives and shook his head. "I can't think of nothing. If she wasn't with me, she was with Bobby, or doing something after school." A small smile bloomed on his tired face. "She was so smart. She was going places." He covered his eyes with his hand, his shoulders heaving.

Seeing Daniel succumb to his emotions triggered something in Shelby's memory. "Daniel, did you send Whitney a mum at school?"

He swallowed and raised his head, trying to pull himself together. "A mum?"

Erickson said, "A flower. For homecoming."

Daniel's face pinched. "I ain't got money for that horseshit. She knew how I felt. I didn't need to send a stupid flower, 'specially not at school."

The front door swung open, and Daniel blinked, wiped his nose on his jacket sleeve, then schooled his features into casual disdain. A tall, lanky man stood in the doorway. He had hair to his shoulders, streaked with gray, and a face full of stubble. His once-white t-shirt was covered in brown stains, and his jeans hung off his lean frame. "What's this then?" He waved his tattooed arms toward the detectives.

"I'm—"

Before Shelby could introduce herself, Daniel said, "Just a couple of asshole truancy officers giving me a hard time."

The man—Daniel's father, Shelby assumed—stepped onto the small porch in front of Daniel and pointed a finger at Shelby. "My son knows more about real life than he can learn in any damn classroom." He rested his hands on his narrow hips. "You're here harrassin' my boy? Ain't you got nothin' better to do?"

"Trust me," Erickson said, "I'd rather be drinking a beer and dipping pretzels in spicy mustard while I watch the Pitt versus Penn State game I've got recorded. But we need to talk to Daniel about—"

Daniel caught Erickson's eye with a look of warning.

"About his assignments in Mr. Long's class. Then we'll be on our way."

Shelby hoped Mr. Mendez would leave them to it, but he refused to budge.

"Go on and git. Leave my kid alone." Daniel's father tapped Daniel's foot with his boot. "C'mon. I'm making grilled cheese." The tall man went back inside the trailer without a word to the detectives. Daniel tossed his cigarette into the sparse grass, shrugged at them, then followed his father into the trailer.

Twenty-Six

Once Shelby and Erickson were on the road, Erickson said, "For a second, I wondered if Daniel's dad could be Whitney's supplier. But there's no way." He held up a finger. "First off, if he had the kind of money a supplier has, he wouldn't live like that." He held up a second finger. "Second, you have to be somewhat organized to run an operation like that. I don't think that guy could run a hot bath."

"He can make grilled cheese." Shelby smirked at Erickson.

He chuckled. "You know what I mean." He held up a third finger. "And finally, that man is definitely not a teddy bear." He squinted as he thought. "More like a scarecrow."

"We shouldn't count him out. Our choices are few and far between. I'll have Naomi run a background check on him, just in case. In the meantime, hopefully, Principal Wheeler opens up and gives us something to work with. Otherwise, we're going to have to get warrants for every red jersey in Locust Grove and try to match it to the fibers forensics has."

Erickson scrubbed his hands over his face. "I don't even want to think about that. I sure wish that brick had given us some DNA. Anything."

"Whoever it was probably wore gloves, like when they killed Whitney."

"You think the brick thrower is the killer?"

"Who else would want to make sure we stay on Bobby, except someone who doesn't want us to continue looking for the murderer?"

Principal Wheeler's house was a modest Cape Cod with a small, but expertly landscaped, yard. A neat pile of russet leaves sat at the curb. They rang the doorbell twice, but no one answered. Erickson peeked through the window of the principal's detached garage. "No car. He must be out."

Shelby called Naomi at the station to get Principal Wheeler's number. Then she phoned him. He was at the school, catching up on work, and could talk to them in his office.

On the way, Erickson said, "I have a lot of respect for educators, but is it normal for a principal to work so much?"

Shelby shrugged and shook her head. "Maybe he's extra busy because it's the start of the school year."

"Or maybe he's doing damage control with the parents Officer Kim told us about."

"Could be."

They parked and Principal Wheeler met them in the hallway like he had on their first visit. The school was empty. He wore a polo shirt, jeans, and spotless sneakers. Shelby noticed he was very fit and moved with the ease of an athlete. He must work out as intensely as he did back in his football days—like Erickson.

Principal Wheeler also had pouches under his bloodshot eyes. In a small town like Locust Grove, an educator's job extended beyond the office into their home. Bellmoor Prep's parents probably called him at all hours.

As he led them to his office, he said, "You might be wondering where all the students are."

Shelby said, "I saw on my news feed that the board voted to close the school and hold virtual classes until the case is solved." They paused outside his office. She continued, "I want to go on record to say that's unnecessary. We don't think someone is targeting students."

Wheeler gave her a tight smile. "But you can't promise that." He led them into his office. They sat in the same places as on their previous visit. Wheeler said, "You don't have to convince me. But it only takes a few hysterical parents to set everyone else shaking in their boots."

"It didn't even happen on school property," Erickson said. "Or during school."

Wheeler shrugged. "Parents turn into mama and papa bears when there's even a hint of danger to their kids." He narrowed his eyes. "What can I do for you, detectives? Are you any closer to arresting someone?" With his right hand, he rubbed his left ring finger where his wedding band used to be.

"Not yet," Shelby replied.

"What about the boyfriend? The last time you were here, you asked me about his history of violence."

"He remains a person of interest," Shelby hedged, "but we're pursuing other leads right now."

The principal sat forward in his armchair and ran his hand through his hair. "You need to wrap this up. Parents are calling me night and day. My email inbox is full of threats to pull kids from Bellmoor Prep. At this rate, the school will close if you don't put someone behind bars and put their minds at ease."

Shelby shared a look with Erickson. The principal's demeanor had roughened since the last time they spoke with him.

She said, "I imagine it's exhausting and frustrating trying to manage them."

"Next time," Erickson spoke up, "just tell them to call the station. There's nothing you can do for them, anyway."

While Erickson smiled affably at the principal, Shelby pressed her lips into a line and knocked Erickson's knee with her own. He looked at her, startled, then realized what he had said. "Not that we can give them any information." His words faded into silence at the end.

"We're here to ask you," Shelby sat forward, "a few more questions."

"Fire away." He waved his hand, indicating she should proceed.

"We've learned that Tom Long was on probation for drinking and for fraternizing with another teacher on school property."

Wheeler leaned back in his chair. "Yes, that's true."

"You didn't mention that when we talked to you before."

He shrugged. "Why would I? It had nothing to do with Whitney."

"No," Erickson leaned forward, clasping his hands between his knees, "but he was pretty chummy with her."

Wheeler nodded. "He was her Quiz Bowl coach."

"He recorded TikToks with her."

Wheeler chuckled. "Are you trying to insinuate something about my teacher?"

"No." Shelby noticed his deflection. "But is it common for teachers to record social media videos with their students?"

"Are you on social media much, Detective?"

"No."

Wheeler nodded. "I wouldn't say it's common, but it's not unusual enough to be a red flag." He crossed his legs, ankle on knee. "Tom has a drinking problem, true. And I'm keeping a close eye on him. But he's not a pedophile, if that's what you're implying. I wouldn't have taken him to the conference with me if I didn't think he's an excellent teacher."

Shelby nodded, noting Wheeler's casual attitude. "We also want to ask you more about Whitney. We've discovered that she sold drugs to students here at Bellmoor Prep."

Wheeler's eyes widened. "Whitney? Whitney Chandler? You must be mistaken. She was a model student."

"That may be," Shelby continued, "but we know for a fact she was selling prescription drugs that are popular with high school students. Like Adderall."

Wheeler ran his hand through his hair again. "I knew Whitney. We worked together closely because of the tutoring program and all the clubs and after-school activities she had. She was at the top of her class. She did the morning announcements." He said this as if the pronouncement settled everything.

"Regardless, we have the evidence. We want to know who she sold to, who supplied her."

He held his hands wide. "How would I know? I know nothing about it. I'm not even sure I believe you."

He stood from his chair and went to the shelves on the far wall, where he took down a framed photo. He gave it to Shelby. In the photo, Wheeler was shaking Whitney's hand and giving her a blue ribbon. A science project sat behind them on a table. Whitney looked proud in her school uniform; her eyes bright. "There's no way the girl in that picture sold drugs, and anyone who told you she did is a liar."

"We have evidence that Whitney sold prescription drugs." Shelby pulled out her notebook and pen. "We're not interested in the students who were buying. At least, not right now. Right now, we're trying to track down her supplier. It's possible he knows something."

"Or he's the killer," Erickson added.

Wheeler paled. "You're serious. You think Whitney was selling drugs?"

"Like I said," Shelby repeated, "we have evidence."

The principal ran his hand through his hair, blowing out a long breath. "What do you want from me?" His bloodshot eyes bounced between Shelby and Erickson.

"I know it's a difficult topic, but are there any parents—men, particularly,—who Whitney was close to?"

Erickson spread his hands in front of him. "Anyone you see her talking with, at games or other school events?"

Wheeler shrugged. "Bobby's parents, obviously. Sometimes Del's. But that makes sense. Wait—" He held out a hand, as if to stop them from rising, although they hadn't moved. "You don't think one of their fathers was Whitney's supplier?"

Shelby made a note. "At this point, we're looking at any male with children."

"Why?"

Shelby squinted at Wheeler. "Information we've gathered is leading us in that direction."

"Like what?"

Shelby shared another look with Erickson. She understood Wheeler was strung out with stress and exhaustion, but surely he knew they couldn't share details of the investigation with him.

He noticed their glances and said as much, practically reading her mind. "Sorry. I know you probably can't tell me. I just need this wrapped up so the students and their parents can get on with their lives."

"And you," Shelby said.

"Yes. Absolutely." He nodded.

Shelby's eyes took in the trophies, award plaques, and framed photos again. Principal Wheeler had lived a charmed life. Whitney's death was probably the worst situation he'd ever faced, especially because they didn't have answers. If they'd already arrested the murderer, he could at least assure the parents that their children were safe. She noticed the football jerseys again, and her stomach dropped through her feet as she realized something. "Mr. Wheeler, can anyone purchase a jersey to support the team? Or are they only distributed to players?"

Her subject change seemed to throw him. He blinked and looked over his shoulder at the framed jerseys. "In years past, only the players received jerseys. But at some point, one of the booster club parents had the brilliant idea of selling them, to raise money for the team. Now, anyone can buy a jersey with any player's number."

Erickson said, "Is there a way to distinguish between the players' jerseys and fan jerseys? Are they made of different material, for instance?"

"Same material," Wheeler replied, "but the school's logo is embroidered on the players' jerseys. The fan jerseys just have iron-on patches."

"Same material." Erickson closed his eyes, no doubt thinking the same thing as Shelby was. That the number of jerseys hanging in closets all around Locust Grove just doubled, or more.

Shelby finished taking a note, then said, "As the principal, you must hear rumors and gossip. Can you think of anything you've heard that could point us toward her supplier? If not a parent, then what about the teachers?"

"The teachers?" Wheeler's eyebrows almost touched his hairline. "Now you're accusing my faculty of being drug dealers?"

Erickson gave him a sympathetic smile. "We're just trying to find answers. It's possible a teacher saw or heard something that could help us. I mean, they saw her every day, right?"

Wheeler's shoulders settled. "That's true."

"Can we get a student directory and a list of Bellmoor Prep faculty members?" Shelby made another note. "Might as well get a list of staff, too. I know when I was in school, the secretary knew everything that went on."

Wheeler rose from his chair. "Good point." He rounded his desk and sat. The detectives waited while he printed copies of the faculty and staff rosters. Then he stood and handed the lists to Erickson, who handed them to Shelby. Wheeler said, "I'll email you the website for the student directory, along with a username and password."

Shelby folded the staff and faculty lists. "Thank you."

"I know you can't share details of the investigation," Wheeler said, "but I'd appreciate an update when you have one. Anything I can tell the parents would be helpful."

Shelby had no intention of updating Wheeler. He would find out when the case was closed at the same time as the rest of Locust Grove. "Thank you for your help." She took a last look at his Bellmoor Bobcats jersey, feeling defeated. Maybe they would have to round up every single jersey in Locust Grove.

Twenty-Seven

Shelby approached Naomi's desk, where the petite woman had her nose pressed nearly to her computer monitor. "Officer Kim."

Naomi slowly raised her head, reluctantly pulling her eyes from whatever she was reading. "Yes, Detective?"

Shelby glanced at the monitor. "Anything new?"

Naomi swept a lock of dark hair behind her ear. "Yes, but not much." She pointed at her monitor. "I was just doing the background check on Tom Long." She shook her head. "Nothing. Also," she clicked her mouse and brought up her email inbox. "Videos are coming in from people who live on Whitney's predicted path between Bobby's and the pool. It was pretty dark, but there are occasional flashes of her."

"Really?" Shelby hadn't expected those videos to give them anything. A zing of hope ran through her. "And?"

Naomi's grim expression quickly dulled that zing. "Nothing new. Her timeline tracks with what everyone told us. She left Bobby's around midnight and headed to the pool. Of course, we don't have any videos of her arriving at the pool."

"How close do we get?"

"We received a video from the Louderback bird feeder, about halfway between Bobby's and the pool." After a few clicks, Naomi brought up a blurry black and white video that showed a girl with long blonde hair walk about five yards from the camera. "You can't see her face, but who else would it be?"

"I don't like to presume anything, but you're right about two things." Naomi raised her eyebrows. "One, these videos don't tell us much and two, that's probably Whitney." Naomi's cheeks pinked with pride. The young officer was turning out to be quite an asset. "What do you know about Daniel Mendez's father?" She felt Erickson come up behind her. She glanced over her shoulder. He was eating a Snickers bar. He grinned at her. She swung her attention back to Naomi.

"I can pull his records for you."

"He's got priors?" Erickson crumpled the Snickers wrapper and dropped it in Naomi's trash can.

Naomi nodded. "Oh, yeah. He's a hot mess."

Shelby rested her hip on Naomi's desk. "Then pull his records, but I also want your take on him."

Naomi sat up, smoothing her hands along her thighs. "Well, he's a drunk, and not a nice one. Everyone knows he beats Daniel's mom, and Daniel, when he was a kid. I think Daniel's too big for that now. Would probably give as good as he got."

"You said he's a hot mess." Erickson crossed his arms, taking a wide stance. "Just domestic violence, or is he into any other criminal activity?"

Naomi looked up at Erickson with puppy dog eyes. Shelby suppressed a groan. "He's got a lot of traffic violations, but he never pays the fines. He's got a lawyer who always shows up and gets the penalties waived." Naomi shook her head. "I don't know how he can afford it."

Shelby had seen how Damien Mendez lived. She, too, wondered how he could afford anyone other than a public defender. "Where does he work?"

"Sparky's Garage."

"He's a mechanic?"

"I don't think so. He drives the tow truck." Naomi glanced at Erickson again, touching her hair.

He looked at his watch. "I think we've got time to drop by."

Shelby nodded. "Thank you, Officer Kim. If you could have his file on my desk when I get back, I'd appreciate it."

The young officer's smile was bright. "You bet, Detective."

Sparky's was in a rundown section of Locust Grove, next to the junkyard. Its once-white cinderblock walls were covered in grime and orange soot from the steel mills that shut down decades before. The name of the garage was painted in a curly font across the front, but the edges were peeling, and the red letters had faded to a dusty pink. Two cars sat on lifts inside the garage, but Shelby didn't see anyone working. Garages were usually full of clanking sounds, blaring music, and deep chatter. Sparky's was silent.

The detectives strolled up to one of the lifted cars, a late-model burgundy Honda Accord. Tools and equipment sat neatly around the floor, which was blotched with oil and grease stains.

Shelby walked into the office, just off the garage bays. Piles of paper blanketed the chipped gray metal desk. A torn rolling chair sat behind the desk, while a stained wooden chair sat in front of it. Outdated calendars and promotional posters that featured buxom women in bikinis, who seemed to enjoy sucking red lollipops, hung on the walls.

"Hello?" Shelby called.

Erickson joined her in the office. "Was there a zombie apocalypse, and we missed it?"

"Can I help you?" A raspy voice piped up behind them. Shelby was thankful she hadn't startled. That's never a good look for a detective.

They turned to find Daniel Mendez's father. He wore greasy blue overalls with his name, Damien, embroidered above his heart. His stringy hair was pulled into a thin ponytail.

"Oh, it's you." He pulled a pack of cigarettes and a lighter from his pocket. His hands were rough and red from a life of manual labor.

He lit one, blowing smoke in their faces. "If Daniel's skipping school again, I don't give a shit."

Shelby waved a hand in front of her face. "We're not truant officers, Mr. Mendez."

"Oh, 'Mister' is it?" His dark eyes crinkled as he took another drag. "If you're not truant officers, who the hell are you?"

"I'm Detective Shelby Reed and this," she gestured to her partner, "is Detective Jasper Erickson. We—"

"What the hell kind of name is Jasper?" Mendez chuckled.

Erickson ignored him. "We'd like to ask you some questions about your son's relationship with Whitney Chandler."

"And your whereabouts around midnight last Friday night," Shelby added, only glancing at Erickson when he threw her a confused look.

Mendez sucked in more smoke, this time blowing it off to the side. "Who's Whitney Chandler?"

Shelby brought out her phone and pulled up a photo of Whitney. Showing it to Mendez, she said, "She was a student at Bellmoor Prep."

Mendez peered at the photo, a lurid grin spreading across his face. "My son's hittin' that? The apple don't fall far, you know what I mean?" He tipped his chin at Shelby.

Her jaw tightened. "She's dead."

Mendez raised his eyebrows. "You think my boy killed her?"

"We're just here to ask some questions."

Mendez threw his cigarette to the cement floor and ground it out with the heel of his boot. "You can ask all the questions you like. I don't got any answers."

Erickson sucked in a breath. "You can answer our questions here, all friendly like, or we can take it to the station." He shook his head, wearing a mocking smile. "No smoking, though."

Mendez threw his hands wide. "It ain't that I don't want to answer your questions. I don't know anything about that girl." He pointed to where Shelby's phone hung at her side. "First time I ever laid eyes on her." He shoved his hands in his pockets. "It's not like Danny brings girls home. We ain't the kind of family to have heart to hearts, if you know what I mean."

Shelby looked past Mendez into the garage bays. "Working alone today?"

Mendez sucked on his teeth. "Nah. Everyone's on break."

Something pulled at Shelby's gut. She believed Mendez that he didn't know anything about Daniel's relationship with Whitney; he didn't seem to recognize her at all from the photo. But something was off, whether with him or the garage or both. She couldn't put her finger on it.

"Where were you Friday night, around midnight?"

Mendez's laugh sounded like sandpaper scraping over metal. "Now you think I killed that girl? I told you, I don't even know her." He rubbed a hand over his chin. "You're not too good at your job, are you, sweetheart?"

Erickson dropped his hands to his side. "Just answer the detective's question."

Mendez eyed them both. "I was at Rivers Casino."

"In Pittsburgh?"

"You know another one?" Mendez pulled out another cigarette and lit it, blowing smoke toward his feet.

Shelby asked, "What time did you leave?"

After another drag, he said, "Can't remember exactly. Maybe one?"

"Which would have put you home around two," Erickson said.

Mendez squinted at him. "Probably."

"Can your wife confirm that?"

Another dry laugh from Mendez. "Wife? My old lady and I ain't married. I'm not that stupid."

Irritation scraped over Shelby's nerves. "Regardless," Shelby said, "can she confirm what time you were home?"

Mendez pinched off his cigarette, sliding the butt back into the carton. "I've answered enough questions. If you want anything else, you'll have to talk to my lawyer."

Erickson huffed, an amused look on his face. "Your lawyer? For a few simple questions about a girl you claim you don't even recognize?"

"Like I said," Mendez bit out. "You'll have to talk to my lawyer. I have to get back to work." He straightened to his full height, which was nearly as tall as Erickson, although his frame was wiry compared to Erickson's muscular one.

"We'll leave you to it," Shelby said, pulling out a business card. "But here's my card if you think of anything." She held it out to him. He looked at the card like she was handing him something from her cat's litter box, but he took it and slid it into his pocket.

In the car, Shelby started the engine and said, "This is the part of the job I hate."

Clicking his seatbelt, Erickson asked, "Which part?"

"Kicking over rocks to see what slithers out." Mendez glared at them through the filthy office window. "Even if he's got nothing to do with Whitney, he's still slimy."

Twenty-Eight

"Give me a second." Shelby held up a finger to Erickson to slow him down as they walked back to her car. He lifted his chin in agreement and waited. She tapped a contact on her phone. Naomi answered. "Officer Kim, I need you to check security footage of the Rivers Casino in Pittsburgh for the night Whitney was murdered."

On the other end of the call, Naomi asked, "What am I looking for?"

"Damien Mendez said he was there that night and didn't leave until one a.m."

There was a pause, probably while Naomi took notes. "Got it. I'll let you know."

"Thanks." She ended the call just as a text came through.

Dad: Hope you wrap up this case soon. My neighbors are asking me questions. You don't want this to hit the news.

She clicked off her phone and continued walking, Erickson by her side. Her father wasn't concerned about her. He was worried a failed investigation would look bad for him.

The wind whipped their hair around their faces. The sky, full of fat clouds, was already darkening thanks to the short autumn day. Soon enough, they would have nightfall before they had their dinners.

Erickson said, "I agree with you. Something's going on with him, but I don't think he killed Whitney. What would be his motive?"

Shelby pulled her hair out of her face. "Maybe he's her supplier. But he doesn't fit the profile, if we're going by what Bobby said."

"No." Erickson stared into the distance, eyes roaming over half-bare trees and the steely sky. "But perps have surprised me before."

Shelby drove them back to the station. The bullpen buzzed with quiet conversations and clicking keyboards. As they walked toward the conference room, they passed Will staring at his monitor and Naomi talking on the phone, taking notes.

Shelby stopped at Will's desk. "Officer Simon."

Like Naomi earlier, his gaze drifted from his monitor to Shelby. "Yes?"

"Did you have any luck with the local pharmacies or the hospital?"

He flipped a pen, end over end, with his fingers as he spoke. "Nope. There aren't that many around here, so it didn't take long. None of them had any inventory that went missing, and they all swore they weren't supplying anyone with anything. Other than their customers with prescriptions, obviously."

Shelby turned to Erickson. "Do you think it's worth getting copies of their inventory records? Checking numbers for what's coming in and what's going out?"

"If I may," Will interrupted, sitting straighter.

With raised eyebrows, Shelby said, "Yes?" Erickson pressed a knuckle to his mouth.

Will cleared his throat. "The pharmacists were shaking in their boots. I don't think it would be worth the time to go over their supply records unless it's a last resort."

She held Will's gaze until he reddened slightly. She was fond of both Will and Naomi, but boundaries must be not only established but also enforced. "You have signed statements?"

He nodded vigorously. "I can pull them—"

She held up a hand. "No need. Thank you, Officer Simon. Excellent work."

He relaxed in his chair, nearly sliding to the floor. Erickson chuckled as they walked to the conference room.

They shrugged out of their jackets. Erickson checked his phone while Shelby stared at the whiteboard Naomi had rearranged for them in their absence. Photos of Whitney and every person of interest, many pulled from social media, hung across the top. From there, Naomi had written a detailed timeline, filling in alibis and other pertinent information and connections between their suspects and Whitney.

"So, Damien was in Pittsburgh at the Rivers Casino. Think he was doing more than gambling? I know he's not a 'teddy bear,' but he's our best bet for Whitney's supplier." Shelby said, still facing the whiteboard.

The corners of Erickson's mouth drew down as he thought. "Possible. It would make sense for whoever was her supplier to have a connection to someone in a larger city, and Pittsburgh is large and close." He leaned back in his chair, tapping his fingers on his knee. "But if he were supplying Whitney, wouldn't Daniel know? Don't you think that would be a reason for some friction between father and son? I haven't seen or heard anything like that."

Shelby sat at the table next to Erickson, her fingers steepled over her waist. "True. But each of them could have been hiding their relationship from the other. Doesn't seem like they have a warm and fuzzy father-son bond." A vision of Shelby's own father popped into her head, a perpetually dismissive look on his face.

"No kidding." Erickson propped his feet on the table. "I remember when I was in middle school. I had a massive crush on this cheerleader. Couldn't stop talking about her. On the way home from football practice one night, my dad gave me 'the talk.' God, it was so embarrassing. For both of us. He kept his eyes on the road the whole time. His face was bright red." Erickson laughed. "Mine probably was, too."

Shelby smiled. "Did you end up dating the cheerleader?"

Erickson shook his head. "Nah. I didn't hit my growth spurt until my freshman year of high school. She didn't look at lil' ol' me twice. What about you?" He raised his eyebrows. "Were you a heartbreaker?"

A snort escaped before she could stop it. "Are you kidding? I hit my growth spurt early, so I was at least a head taller than most of the boys."

"Ouch."

"Exactly." She shook her head. "No one wants to dance with an Amazon, even if their line of sight was my chest."

Erickson chuckled just as Naomi whooshed into the room, a file in hand. "What's up, Officer Kim?"

She was so full of energy she bounced on her toes. Shelby wondered if it was enthusiasm or caffeine.

"I checked with Rivers Casino in Pittsburgh."

Shelby's eyebrows lifted. "That was fast."

Naomi shrugged, looking smug. "I know a guy. Went to high school with him."

Erickson frowned. "You went to high school with a lot of people for such a small town."

"Well," Naomi shifted to face him. "When you go to school around here, you go to school with not just the people in their class, but everyone in their families, you know?"

He nodded. "Gotcha."

"Anyway, I had them email you the video files," she nodded to Shelby. "They should already be in your inbox. And here's Damien Mendez's file." She placed it on the table before rounding the end to stand behind Shelby. Erickson joined her. Shelby popped open her laptop and opened her email. Sure enough, a new message was waiting. However, she had forgotten what a big operation Rivers Casino was and how many cameras the business had focused on the entrances and exits.

She rubbed her forehead. "There are six files per hour, one for each camera."

"I can review them," Naomi said. "Just forward them to me. I'll split them between me and Will." She glanced into the bullpen. "If I can pull him away from forensics long enough." She giggled, then stopped, a blush creeping over her high cheekbones. She glanced at Shelby, who pursed her lips, then Erickson, who smiled and winked. Then she scurried back to her desk, her dark hair falling forward to hide her face.

Shelby leaned back in her chair, her hands folded over her stomach. "Do I need to have a word with Officer Simon?"

Erickson sat again, sliding the Mendez file toward him. "Maybe. I don't mind a little office gossip, and I certainly don't begrudge the dude some romance, but the last thing we need is any suggestion from outside the station that forensics is distracted or not concentrating on the case." He noticed the look of surprise on Shelby's face. "What? You're not the only one who thinks about optics." He crossed his arms over his chest.

They held each other's eyes for a moment. A familiar comfort settled across Shelby's shoulders, relaxing her muscles. Erickson was becoming a partner she could trust, a partner she could count on. It had been a long time since she'd felt that kind of comradery, on the same page as her partner, focused on a single mission. She hoped that feeling wasn't misleading, that she could trust it as well as Erickson.

"Okay, story time." He opened the Mendez file. His blonde eyebrows rose to his hairline. "Naomi was right. His list of priors is impressive."

Shelby closed her laptop and sat forward. "Hit me."

"Lots of B and E in his teen years, small-time theft. In and out of juvie until he aged out." He flipped a page, and his brow furrowed. "Then he graduated to boosting cars."

"Was he convicted?"

"Yep." Erickson turned the page over, then back again. "Sentenced to five years, out in three."

"And then?"

"It's like Naomi said. He gets arrested, shows up in court with an attorney, and either the judge drops the charges or fines him and sends him on his way."

"Who's the attorney?"

Erickson slid the pages around until he found the answer. "Rose Capito."

"We should talk to her."

Erickson checked his watch. "Will have to be tomorrow. Office hours are over." He stood and grabbed his jacket. "Dinner?"

Twenty-Nine

Shelby and Erickson stood at Gino's chrome counter and stared at the menu hanging from the ceiling. Shelby couldn't find a single healthy food listed. The only vegetables were fried or toppings on a pizza. She settled on the eggplant parmesan hoagie and a bottle of water while Erickson ordered an Italian meatball hoagie with a side of fried mushrooms and a lemonade. His A1C must be ridiculous, besides his cholesterol levels.

They took seats in a booth under a framed Oak Glen Golden Bears jersey. Local high school sports jerseys hung on every wall. Trophies and autographed balls sat on shelves here and there. Erickson stared with childlike fascination while Shelby unfolded her napkin and set her plastic utensils on the table.

Her phone buzzed. She pulled it from her bag and saw her father was calling. She silenced it and set it face down on the table. When Erickson lifted his eyebrows, she shook her head and said, "Did you have dreams of the NFL?"

"Of course." He slapped his palms on the table and leaned back. "Any kid who plays a sport dreams of going pro. At least until it becomes clear they're not good enough."

"When does that happen?" A server placed a bottle of water in front of her, lemonade in front of Erickson, then darted away.

He blew out his lips. "Depends on your natural ability. Some kids realize early on they're not fast enough or strong enough or don't have great hand-eye coordination. Others, like me, don't realize until it's time for the draft and they haven't heard a peep."

She took a sip and frowned. "Surely the coaches give you some idea."

He popped the straw in his mouth, sucking and nodding. "Yeah, but that doesn't mean you always believe them. Don't get me wrong." He held up his hands. "I wasn't heartbroken or anything." He slurped. "Well, maybe a little." A wink.

She almost smiled. His winks were growing on her, but she would never let him know. "Why did you decide to go into law enforcement?"

He groaned and scrubbed his face. "Would you believe it was because of a woman?"

She snorted, surprising herself and Erickson. The weight of the investigation that had been pressing down on her lifted a little. "Yes, actually, I would believe it. Do tell."

He scrunched his face and spun his lemonade cup in his hands. "A girl I dated briefly in college majored in psychology."

"Of course she did." Shelby had majored in criminal justice, thinking psychology was too soft for police work. After befriending a few psychology majors, she knew she'd chosen wisely.

"And she was accepted into the academy. I majored in—"

"Don't tell me." She put a finger to her temple. "Phys ed."

He pressed his lips together. "No. Business." When Shelby gave him a questioning look, he said, "I figured I'd need to know how to manage my pots of money after going pro."

"Ah."

"At the very least, the sales skills would come in handy when I filmed commercials for my lucrative sponsorship deals." He flashed her a charming smile.

"I see." She bit the inside of her lip to keep from grinning.

Erickson narrowed his eyes. "C'mon, you've been twenty. Don't you remember what it was like, Detective?"

She cleared her throat. "Sorry. I've always been down-to-earth." A memory of her father dropping her off on campus, with barely a wave before leaving, popped up in her mind. She blinked it away.

"Anyhoo." He took a drink. "Once my dream of being drafted to the NFL went bust, I had daydreams of my girlfriend and me fighting crime together."

Shelby's shoulders shook from the effort not to laugh out loud. "A regular Benson and Stabler."

He clasped his hands on the table, looking indignant. "I'll have you know Law & Order: SVU was my favorite TV show."

Her laughter finally escaped. It felt good, sending a fizzy feeling through her chest and down her limbs.

Erickson said, "What about you?"

Her phone vibrated on the table. She shoved it back in her bag. "What?"

"What led you into law enforcement?"

She took a big swig of water. Replacing the cap on the bottle, she said, "My mom."

"Your mom was a police officer?"

"No, no." She picked at the label of her bottle. "She was in marketing. No, my mom was killed by a drunk driver when I was in high school." Her eyes stayed fixed on the bottle. "It wasn't his first DUI. He belonged to the country club." She met Erickson's eyes, which were full of sympathy. "So did the judge." She dropped her eyes again, but not before catching a tick in Erickson's jaw. "I was furious. My father," she blew out through her nose, "said that's how the game is played." She pushed her bottle aside and dropped her hands to her lap, meeting Erickson's incredulous gaze. "I told him it wasn't a game, and he laughed." His jaw ticked again. "I decided to become a cop then and there, not just to change the game, to eliminate it."

Silence ticked by as they stared at each other. Shelby felt them cross an imaginary threshold into a new territory in their partnership. She welcomed the shift, and that surprised her.

Before she could ask another question, a voice next to her growled, "How dare you?" Shelby looked up into the twisted, angry face of Lisa Chandler and the feeling vanished. "How dare you drag our daughter's name through the mud." Shelby could see Jeremy Chandler standing behind his wife, gaze on the floor, hands twitchy at his sides.

"Mrs. Chandler—"

"Look." Mrs. Chandler slammed her hand and something else on the table in front of Shelby. Shelby reluctantly moved her focus from the grief-stricken woman next to her to the table. When Mrs. Chandler lifted her shaking hand, Shelby saw the front-page headline of Locust Grove's newspaper: "Dead Girl Dealt Drugs."

Fury ignited in Shelby's chest for two reasons. First, the department clearly had a leak who was feeding information to the newspaper and to whoever threw the brick into her house. Second, the public would have a field day with this headline, sending the station's tip line into a frenzy, and creating a mess of gossip and rumors for them to sift through.

She spun the newspaper on the table for Erickson to see. He closed his eyes. Mrs. Chandler was breathing hard, her eyes wild and wet with tears.

Shelby tried again. "Mrs. Chandler—"

"Take it back." Mrs. Chandler's spittle landed on Shelby's cheek. She flinched, but didn't move to wipe it. "Call the paper and tell them it isn't true. That you planted the evidence because you're so desperate—" more spittle, "to cross my girl off your to-do list, and you have no idea who killed her."

Erickson stood, holding up placating hands. "We didn't plant that evidence."

"Take it back!" Mrs. Chandler pressed herself into Erickson's face. He stood his ground, compassion filling his eyes.

The workers and the other customers stared at the miserable group, mouths agape. Shelby spotted someone recording the scene with their phone. She squeezed out of the booth to stand, blocking the camera's view and glaring at its owner. She threw a pleading glance at Mr. Chandler. He pressed his lips together, unshed tears shining in his eyes, too. For a moment, Shelby thought he would join his wife in the shouting. But he reached out and gently took his wife's arm in his hand. "Lisa."

She shook him off and faced Shelby again. "You're through. You and your partner. I'll get you fired. Then the paper will be full of headlines about you." She nearly spat the last word. "And dirty cops. And how my bright, beautiful girl..." She choked on the end of her sentence, dissolving into tears.

"Honey, let's go." Mr. Chandler placed one arm over his wife's shoulder, the other around her elbow. "You said your piece. Time to go." She leaned into her husband, much like she did when Shelby broke the news of their daughter's murder to them. He glared at Shelby, but led his wife out of the restaurant.

Shelby and Erickson took their seats. The server silently placed their food in front of them and scurried away quickly. The customers stared. Shelby met each of their gazes until they went back to their own dinners. She pulled her phone from her bag, her guts squirming. Now she knew why her father had been calling. To warn her.

Thirty

That night, once Shelby was wrapped in the fleecy warmth of her bed and Queenie curled into her side, she opened her laptop to examine the report on Whitney that Erickson filed. The frigid air that had slithered around her feet and twined around her shoulders was gone, thanks to the new glass pane in her bay window. She logged into the department's secure site and clicked until the report opened. She skimmed the basic information that they filled in for every report, then landed on Erickson's notes. His reasons for naming Bobby Garza as the primary suspect were sound, at the time. And he had listed the other persons of interest in their investigation, namely Tom Long. He had also described the evidence they'd found in Whitney's room.

Someone who had access to their system easily could have read this report and leaked vital information, which might have led to the brick through her window and the headline in the newspaper. But who? Who on their team would jeopardize their investigation? Shelby couldn't imagine Naomi or Will was a mole. Both young officers were keen to move up the ranks. And she trusted Erickson, even though her faith in him was only recently solidified. The captain? That made even less sense.

She considered updating the report, but decided it was in the investigation's interest to keep new information out of the system. Eventually, Captain Guerrero would want it updated, but until then, the current report could stand. Shelby didn't want another leak. Let the mole think they were at a standstill.

Shelby closed the report and went to the Locust Grove Gazette website. The headline about Whitney still sat above the fold. She scanned the article, noticing that it was short and offered little insight into the case. Mrs. Chandler was quoted, however, saying, "I don't know why the police are bound and determined to drag Whitney's name through the mud. But I'll tell you this: Our daughter didn't do drugs, and she definitely didn't sell them." Rather than get angry at Mrs. Chandler's accusation, Shelby's heart broke for the woman. She understood the need to lash out, to strike at the nearest target when a loved one is taken away so suddenly, so violently.

Shelby sighed and closed her laptop, prompting Queenie to open one baleful eye. She stroked the cat's head, and Queenie went back to sleep, while Shelby stared at the pattern of her bedspread and thought about their suspects, or lack thereof. Bobby and Del were cleared. Tom Long and Damien Mendez didn't fit the usual profile of a dealer. But Tom Long's creepy relationship with Whitney didn't help him, and Damien was definitely hiding something. Both of them had dubious alibis confirmed only by their significant others. Once Naomi scoured the videos from the casino, they'd know more about Damien.

If Whitney's death wasn't tied to drugs, then what was the motive? Was there a piece they were missing? A part of Whitney's life that was yet to be revealed?

Mrs. Chandler's face, twisted in anger, loomed in Shelby's mind. How long until the national news picked up on their small-town investigation? The murder of a pretty young white girl was a gold mine for twenty-four-hour news channels. They would dig into Whitney's life, interview her parents, her friends. Video footage of Bellmoor Prep would run under voiceovers describing how Whitney was found, along with questions about security and safety in Locust Grove. Inevitably, Guerrero would have to give a statement to the press, which would lead to camera operators and newscasters with microphones chasing Shelby and Erickson, impeding their progress.

She was spiraling, and she knew why. Her past was intruding on her present, like a film negative layered over the reel that was currently playing. Except there were differences between the past and present. She needed to hold on to those differences to ground herself in reality.

She closed her eyes and filled her lungs, releasing the breath on a slow count of five. Tomorrow she would get answers, fill in the blanks on Tom Long, Damien Mendez, and the department's mole. In the meantime, getting a solid night's sleep was all she could do for Whitney. She turned off her bedside lamp, slid under the covers, and drifted off with Queenie's soft purring in her ears.

* * *

"Detective Reed." Naomi nearly launched out of her chair to meet Shelby at the entrance to the bullpen. Will wasn't far behind her. They seemed to jockey for position.

"Officers." Shelby injected her greeting with a light warning to behave. They immediately ceased elbowing each other. "The two of you are bright-eyed and bushy-tailed this morning. Is there a reason?"

"Oh, yeah, there is," Will almost shouted, to drown out Naomi's polite, "Yes, Detective Reed."

Shelby eyed both of them before saying to Naomi, "Explain."

Naomi's face lit up like a kid at a carnival, while Will's shoulders slouched. She said, "Last night, around one a.m., one of the uniformed officers who was positioned at the intersection of—"

"We've got Damien Mendez in a cell," Will interrupted. Naomi glared at him, her mouth agape. "What?" He shrugged. "You were taking too long to get to the point."

Shelby rubbed a finger between her eyebrows. "Why is Damien Mendez in a cell?"

Before Naomi or Will could say anything, Erickson, hidden from view, piped up from the conference room. "He got pulled over late last night on a D.U.I."

Shelby's eyebrows lifted, and a smile tugged at one corner of her mouth. After last night's fruitless ruminations, Shelby was happy to have a new knot to unravel that might lead to some answers. She left Naomi and Will in the bullpen and strode into the conference, adrenaline shooting through her veins. She said, "Tell me what happened."

Erickson, wiping powdered sugar from his mouth with a paper napkin, swiveled in his chair to face her. "He was on his way back from Pittsburgh when a uniform clocked him going twenty over the speed limit just off the exit ramp. He blew through the red light, too."

Shelby leaned her hip against the conference table. "How high was his blood alcohol level?"

Erickson slid a mug—her "On the Case" mug—of hot coffee toward her. "Twice the legal limit. But hold on—" He took a sip from his own mug that said, "This guy is awesome," with an arrow pointing up. "He was towing a car."

Shelby huffed in disbelief, almost choking on her hot coffee. "He was towing a car? Speeding? And drunk?" She toasted Erickson with her mug. "Thanks for this."

Erickson held his mug in two hands and frowned. "The coffee or the news?"

She cocked her head, then said, "Both, actually." She set her mug on the table. "We can use this as leverage. Make him answer a few questions."

He pointed at her. "Great minds run alike."

Shelby turned toward the open conference room door. "Officer Kim, can you join us?" Naomi hurried into the room, notepad and pen at the ready. Shelby said, "What did you find in the video footage from the casino security cameras?"

Naomi tapped her pen against the notepad. "Unfortunately, nothing. Mr. Mendez is telling the truth. The video shows him exiting the parking garage just before one a.m."

"Thank you, Officer."

Naomi disappeared back into the bullpen. According to forensics, Whitney died around twelve-thirty in the morning. Mendez was still at the casino when Whitney was killed. Although the time of death could be slightly sooner or later, it looked like Mendez was covered.

Erickson clasped his hands behind his head and leaned back. "I haven't even told you the best part."

Still working through Mendez and his alibi, distracted, Shelby said, "There's more?"

Erickson gave her a slow nod. "The car he was towing is stolen."

Shelby's grin spread from ear to ear. Erickson looked taken aback, no doubt because he'd never seen her smile like that. Then he mirrored her expression.

They could still make Mendez sweat. She said, "And it's not even nine o'clock."

Erickson lifted his drink. "The mug says it all. I'm awesome."

Thirty-One

Damien Mendez drew invisible circles on the table in the interrogation room with his finger. He looked like he didn't have a care in the world, regardless that he was handcuffed to the D-ring in the middle of the steel table.

Shelby turned on the recording equipment and gave the legally required introduction. Then she clasped her hands on the table and watched Damien. Erickson, sitting to her left, had his arms crossed. His knee bounced under the table. She itched to push her leg against his, to quiet him, because she had the sense that Damien was smarter than he looked. She didn't want to give anything away.

Damien finally lifted his gaze and met hers. He smirked. "No coffee? Water?"

Rather than answer his question, Shelby said, "Tell us about last night."

"Last night?" His smirk deepened. "Had a great time." He cocked his head to the side. "Until I didn't."

Erickson leaned forward, resting his forearms on the table. "Tell us about the car."

Mendez laughed. "I reckon you know everything there is to know about that car. Why ask me?"

Erickson gave him a smile that was all teeth. "Humor us."

Damien sat up and directed his answer to Shelby, though Erickson had asked the question. "I was towing it."

Shelby said, "From where to where?"

Damien ran his tongue over his teeth. "Oh, from there to here." He smiled. "I don't think I should say anything else until my lawyer gets here." He leaned back in his chair and drew circles again.

"Okay." Shelby rested her palms on the table. "You don't have to say anything. We'll have you taken back to your cell. According to Ms. Capito's assistant, she's on a digital detox in some cabin at Deep Creek Lake and will be back in a week." She stood, nodding to Erickson that he should do the same, which he did with a shrewd look in his eyes. "I'll have Officer Simon bring you a menu of meals for the week." She tapped the table. "Don't give yourself a paper cut." She walked to the door, Erickson on her heels.

Just as Shelby's hand rested on the doorknob, Mendez said, "What the hell is a digital detox?"

"Oh," Erickson turned back, "it's when someone goes off-grid. No cellphone, no Wi-Fi, no TV, nothing electronic. So, unless Ms. Capito left you a landline number to call?" He held his hands wide and tilted his head back and forth. A muscle near Mendez's left eye twitched. "No? Then we'll see you in a week." He turned his back on Mendez.

But before Shelby could open the door, Mendez growled, "All right. You win. I don't want to spend a week in this shithole waiting on that bitch."

Shelby and Erickson took their seats. Erickson pointed at Mendez. "Watch your language."

Mendez chuckled and tipped his chin toward Shelby. "She's got you on a short leash."

Neither of them took the bait. Shelby asked again, "Where did you pick up the car and where were you taking it?"

Mendez shifted in his chair, twisting his handcuffed wrists. "Picked it up in Pittsburgh. Was taking it to Sparky's."

"For who?"

He sucked on his teeth. "A friend."

Erickson said, "What's your friend's name?"

Mendez continued to twist his hands, one over the other, making the cuffs clink in the quiet while the detectives waited. After several seconds, through gritted teeth, he said, "Look, I'm not the guy you want. I just do what I'm told."

Shelby shared a quick look with Erickson, then said, "What are you told to do?"

Mendez rested his elbows on the table, head in his hands. "This is some horse shit."

Erickson knocked twice on the table. "What are you told to do?"

Mendez looked like he'd swallowed a shot of battery acid. Beads of sweat glistened on his twisted upper lip. "If I talk, can I get some kind of immunity?"

Both Shelby and Erickson knew they had no authority to offer Mendez any immunity from prosecution or to reduce a sentence. But they also knew they could blur the lines in an interrogation to get what they needed.

Shelby said, "We can't make any promises." When Mendez muttered a curse, she added, "But I will go to bat for you if you come clean." She leaned toward Mendez. The faint odor of stale cigarette smoke, whiskey, and acrid flop sweat greeted her. "We need answers. You're still a suspect in the murder of Whitney Chandler."

Mendez huffed a mirthless laugh. "I told you I was at the casino until one."

Erickson said, "Time of death is tough to determine in cold weather. You might have had time to leave the casino, meet up with Whitney, and strangle that poor girl to death."

Sweat slicked Mendez's forehead. "I told you. I didn't even know that chick."

"You've got a long list of priors, Mr. Mendez." Shelby leaned back, crossing her legs. "Including domestic abuse, which ties in nicely with Whitney's cause of death. And we need to wrap up that case. It wouldn't be hard for us to give the D.A. a convincing report naming you as our main suspect." She glanced at Erickson, who nodded in agreement, playing his part. "With your reputation in Locust Grove, it wouldn't take much persuasion on the D.A.'s part to get a jury to convict you." She shrugged. "Life in prison for a crime you didn't commit?"

Mendez's nostrils flared. "My lawyer would never let it get that far. You're making up shit."

"What if," Erickson squinted at the ceiling, "whoever you're working for decides you're not worth the effort? You're sitting in jail. What if they don't want to spend the money to get you out because it's easier to let you rot behind bars?" He studied Mendez. "I imagine they could replace you pretty easily. Boosting cars isn't an especially skilled trade." He wrinkled his nose. "And getting arrested with said boosted car? Kind of makes you a liability, doesn't it?"

Mendez ran a grimy hand over his mouth. His eyes bulged slightly. He seemed to mull over Erickson's scenario, possibly worrying he was right.

In a soft voice, Shelby said, "Tell us what you're told to do, Mr. Mendez. And who's telling you to do it."

Mendez melted into the back of his chair, his face slack. He hung his head. "His name is Keith Crabtree."

That name wasn't on Shelby's radar. A boss's reputation usually preceded him. Shelby glanced at Erickson, who shrugged. "Is he from Pittsburgh?"

Mendez shook his head. "Baltimore."

Erickson made a noise at the back of his throat. "Ugh. Ravens fan. How did you get hooked up with him?"

"He was at Rivers Casino one night," Mendez said. "We were playing poker." A smile came and went. "It was a good night for me. I was up by five thousand when I walked away from the table." He ran a hand through his unruly hair. "Keith offered to buy me a drink, asked what I did for a living. I told him I drove a tow truck, thinking him in his fancy suit would make some joke. But he was interested. Asked me all kinds of questions. And then he offered me a job." He looked at Shelby. "I took it."

She said, "Stealing cars."

"Not just any cars," he clarified. "I wouldn't have taken the job if I thought I'd get busted. But Crabtree has the perfect operation going. See, there's all these business people who leave their cars parked around Pittsburgh, in the residential areas. Then they have someone take them to the airport from there."

Erickson said, "Free parking."

Mendez nodded. "Right. 'Cause they go on these long trips, months sometimes, and they don't want to pay all that money at the airport parking. So I go around looking for the ones all covered in dust, or snow, in the winter. Sometimes the owners are dead. That's when we hit the jackpot." He gave Erickson a slimy grin.

"But when these people return for their cars," Shelby said, drawing Mendez's attention again, "don't they report their stolen car to the police?"

"That's the beauty of Keith's operation. Most of the time, they think they lost it, can't remember where they parked it. Or," he raised a finger, "it's been so long the cops tell 'em the trail's gone cold and there's no hope of finding it."

Erickson added, "Let alone tracing it to Locust Grove, West Virginia."

Mendez smirked. "No shit. And by then," he spread his fingers where his hands were cuffed, "it's been hacked to parts and sold, anyway. Y bueno."

Shelby sat up, crossed her arms, and leaned on the table. "And the night Whitney died? Were you scouting cars in Pittsburgh?"

Mendez leaned forward, too, assaulting her with his stench. "Yeah. Didn't find any. But I came home with an extra eight hundred bucks in my wallet." He bared his nicotine-stained teeth.

Shelby wondered how much of Mendez's earnings went toward rent or food or clothes for his family. She guessed very little.

"Now," Mendez twisted his wrists inside their handcuffs, "let's talk about immunity."

"Like I said," Shelby rose from her chair, "I'll go to bat for you, but I can't make any promises."

"And like I said," Erickson also stood, "your attorney is gone for a week, so you'll be our guest until she returns, and we can get you transferred to Pittsburgh."

Mendez yanked on his cuffs, the chain rattling against the table. "You can't keep me. I came clean. I gotta get outta here. He'll find me!" His eyes blazed with fear.

Erickson paused at the door. "What was it you said?" He snapped his fingers, a wolfish smile taking over his face. "Oh, right. Y bueno."

The detectives walked out the door, leaving Mendez gaping behind them.

Thirty-Two

Shelby and Erickson stared at the whiteboard in the conference room. They'd removed Damien Mendez's photo and erased his details. Only a few photos remained. They were running out of leads.

Erickson sipped a Mountain Dew from the vending machine. He'd given Shelby a Dasani without a word. They were gelling, but Shelby didn't have the bandwidth to think about the progress of their partnership. Frustration was tightening around her lungs like laces pulled too tight.

"I want to question Tom Long again," she said, taking a cooling sip of water. She was so tense she felt it slide all the way into her stomach. "My gut tells me he's hiding something." She looked at Erickson. "Those phone calls. Maybe we can find out more about those phone calls."

Erickson nodded. "Can't hurt." He was staring at Long's photo on the board. "Hard to believe the school board didn't fire him outright."

Something pricked the back of Shelby's mind. "You're right. Seems like teachers are fired left and right for just about anything these days. Why was he only put on probation?"

"We could ask Wheeler." Erickson brought out his phone and tapped a few times. "According to the paper, all Bellmoor Prep faculty and staff had to report today for an in-service training."

Shelby zipped her jacket and gulped more coffee. "I wonder if Wheeler is briefing them on how to handle hysterical parents."

Erickson downed his Mountain Dew. "I hope, one day, when I have kids, I don't act like a ninny."

Shelby snorted. "A ninny?" She headed toward the parking lot. "Okay, grandpa."

Erickson held the door for her. "Don't sass me, young lady."

Their lightheartedness belied the worry that churned in Shelby's stomach. They needed to arrest someone, and time was running out.

* * *

"Where is everyone?" Erickson stood in the intersection of Bellmoor Prep's hallways, looking left and right.

When they had arrived at the school, the parking lot was empty, but the doors were unlocked. Principal Wheeler wasn't in his office, and they didn't see any teachers.

Shelby looked out the window, toward the center courtyard. "I guess we missed them."

"Why are the doors unlocked if no one's here?"

"Good question." She walked down the hallway opposite from Wheeler's office. The classrooms were dark. She stopped at one and tried the doorknob. Locked. She continued walking.

Next to her, Erickson said, "Look down there."

A shaft of light coming from a classroom bounced off the polished floor. "Someone's still here."

"Maybe the last one here locks up."

They approached the door. Through the window, they saw a woman in a long quilted coat, yoga pants, and sneakers standing at the desk. She was stuffing notebooks into a canvas tote bag that said, "Live, Love, Laugh." The detectives paused outside the door, and when the woman turned to open a drawer, she spotted them and cried out. Putting a hand to her chest, she said, "I'm so sorry. I didn't know anyone was there. You scared me." She opened the door for the detectives, her eyes raking them from head to toe. "You must be the cops working on Whitney's murder." She pressed her lips together and shook her head. "Such a shame."

Shelby walked into the classroom, Erickson following her. "I'm Detective Shelby Reed and this is Detective Jasper Erickson." Her eyes fell on the tote bag. "Are you a teacher here?"

The woman waved a hand. "Oh, no. But my husband is. I'm Nikki Long. My husband, Tom, teaches history here."

"Oh, yes," Shelby said. "We've met your husband."

Mrs. Long smirked at them. "I heard."

"Out of curiosity," Erickson said, "why are you packing up his desk?"

"Oh, I'm not packing up his desk." Mrs. Long held up the canvas tote. "I'm just picking up some work he wants to do at home."

Shelby said, "Why can't he pick it up himself? Is he all right?"

Nikki rolled her eyes. "He's hungover like a daffodil in June. Couldn't be bothered to drag his sorry ass into work, so here I am." She struck a pose like a game show hostess before continuing to pack the tote bag.

Erickson said, "Tied one on last night?"

"Ha. Last night, the night before." She opened a desk drawer and removed a binder. "Don't get me started. Most of the time, he's either drunk or hungover. What good is he to me like that?" Apparently she was so frustrated with Long that she didn't mind, or didn't realize, she was over sharing with the police.

An uneasy sensation tingled over Shelby's scalp. "Do you think he was drunk at the conference? The one in Pittsburgh?"

"Oh, you heard about the conference?" She squinted up at the ceiling. "I guess that makes sense. That was the night Whitney was killed, right? Poor girl." She rested her fist on her hip. "And you can bet dollars to donuts he was drunk."

Shelby took in the classroom. The posters of past presidents, maps, inspirational quotes. "I'm surprised he would get drunk at a work event, and in front of his boss."

"Who, Al? Pfft." She waved a hand in the air. "He doesn't care as long as Tom remembers his place."

"His place?"

"Sure." She stopped packing and fanned her face. "Al likes to play the puppet master, pulling the teacher's strings. As long as Tom plays his game, Al will let him get away with anything."

Erickson said, "But your husband is on probation. Wouldn't drinking—"

Mrs. Long laughed, high and bright, as if they were swapping stories at a cocktail party. "Oh, honey, that was nothing. Al had to file that for the state. But it's convenient for him because he can hold it over Tom, make him dance." She wiggled her fingers as if she were controlling marionettes.

Shelby's mind was racing. "Are you saying Tom would owe him, or he'd lose his job?"

"Bingo." Mrs. Long pointed at Shelby. "He's always calling in little favors from the teachers. Pick up his kids, run an errand, cover for him at a meeting."

"Cover for him?" Shelby's heart rate ticked up. Sweat slicked her palms.

"Oh, yeah. Sometimes he fakes having a sick kid or something to get out of a PTA meeting or teacher-parent conferences. Then he asks a teacher to make up an excuse for him."

Shelby threw a sharp look at Erickson, who stared back at her. She said, "Mrs. Long, can you tell me again when your husband came home from the conference?"

Mrs. Long rolled her eyes. "Not until eleven o'clock Saturday morning, the lazy jerk. He was supposed to take Austin to Quiz Bowl practice so I could go to Pilates, but he was too late."

"If Tom was that drunk the night before, I hope Mr. Wheeler followed him closely on the road, to make sure he got home safely."

"I don't know about that." Mrs. Long hiked the bulging tote bag onto her shoulder. "Far as I know, Al left the night before. I remember because Tom kept bitching about how Al had left him there when he wanted a ride home so he could sleep the whole way."

Electricity sparked down Shelby's spine. She met Erickson's eyes. He felt it, too. Suddenly, the timeline for these two men skewed differently than before.

Mrs. Long wiped her forehead with the back of her hand. "Sorry. I'd like to stay and chat, but I have to get this work home to Tom and make lunch for our son."

Erickson said, "You've been a big help, Mrs. Long." He was out the door in a flash, Shelby on his heels.

Thirty-Three

The detectives retraced their steps back to the principal's office, on the off-chance Wheeler had shown up. It was empty; the door locked.

Erickson paced in front of the door. "He's not here."

Shelby chewed her lip. "Before we go off half-cocked, let's get our ducks in a row and make sure we're on the same page."

Erickson blinked, the hint of a smirk on his lips. "So many idioms in one sentence."

She glared at him, then strode toward the parking lot.

At the station, the scents of coffee, sugar, and lemon furniture polish filled the conference room. Will had taken up Erickson's baton and brought in donuts for everyone. If they continued this way, the Locust Grove police force would become a fat cliché.

Shelby sipped hot coffee. "Wheeler's alibi just got blown out of the water."

Erickson pointed at her with a partially eaten Boston cream donut. When had he picked that up? "We need to bring him in."

Shelby leaned out of the open doorway. "Officer Kim, can you join us?" She spotted Will at his desk, head in his hands. "And Officer Simon?"

When the young officers arrived, notebooks and pens in hand, Shelby said, "Officer Kim, when you confirmed alibis for Tom Long and Alfred Wheeler with the conference hotel, what did you find out?"

Naomi flipped to her notes. "Neither of them checked out in person. They left their room keys in their rooms. The housekeepers found them Saturday morning after the eleven a.m. checkout time." Her eyes bounced between Shelby and Erickson. "Is something wrong?"

"Mrs. Long told us her husband didn't return home until eleven on Saturday morning, but Principal Wheeler wasn't with him. We had assumed, and we shouldn't have, that the two men left the hotel together. Now it seems our timeline is incorrect."

Naomi nodded. "After the hotel receptionist said they didn't check out in person, I asked if they had eaten breakfast there, if there were breakfast charges on their room bills."

Erickson pointed his donut at Naomi. "Good thinking."

"And?" Shelby asked.

Naomi shook her head. "No breakfast charges."

"We need security footage of the parking garage from about dinnertime on Friday through early Saturday morning."

"On it," Naomi said, spinning away toward the bullpen.

"Officer Simon, we need to talk to Tom Long. I'd like you to bring him in. He's not being arrested, but make sure he understands this is a demand and not a request." Will nodded, scowling. She examined him, noticing that his eyes were red. He wasn't bouncing on the balls of his feet or making wisecracks like usual. "Everything all right, Officer Simon?"

Will nodded but didn't meet her eyes. "All good. Just, uh, just a personal matter."

She shared a look with Erickson. "Anything we can help with?"

Will chewed his lip. "Detective Reed, I screwed up."

She sat on the edge of the table, brows furrowed. "What do you mean?"

Will pressed his lips together and looked at her. He glanced at Erickson, who wiped his face with a napkin, then waved his hand for Will to continue. Will sucked in a deep breath. "You know Shane? In forensics?"

Shelby rubbed her temple. The last thing she wanted to do was counsel someone on their love life. The last threads of their investigation were typing up. She could feel it. "Yes."

"I thought I could trust him. I mean, I thought he was one of us."

With sudden clarity, Shelby knew what Will was going to say. Her impatience evaporated as a white-hot ember burned in her chest. "Although he works for us, and his office is in this building, he is a civilian. He didn't take the same oath that you did. That Detective Erickson and I did."

He met her eyes. He looked miserable. "I didn't think about that." He sighed. "I found out... Well, I found out—"

She worked hard, very hard, to keep her voice even. "You found out he's been leaking information about the case."

Erickson audibly swallowed the last bite of his donut.

Will's eyes flew wide, and his mouth hung open. "How did you know?"

Shelby rubbed both of her temples, trying to erase the tension she felt building in her head. "Because we've seen the newspaper. Because someone threw a rock and a note through my front window."

Will hung his head.

Breathing through her nose, she looked at Erickson. His eyes were full of compassion for the young officer. He tipped his chin toward Will, giving her a subtle message.

She cleared her throat. "It's not your fault." Will's head snapped up. She'd never seen such fragile hope in someone's eyes. "Shane signed a confidentiality contract when he took this job. He knew the rules." After a beat, she gave him a small smile. "You did nothing wrong. You thought you were discussing the case with a colleague. He's the one who broke his contract."

Will reached up like he was going to hug her, but when he saw the horror on her face, he crossed his arms over his chest. He blinked. "Thank you. You don't know how relieved I am to—"

"But in the future," she raised her finger, "trust no one until they give you a reason to trust them." She threw a quick look at Erickson and regretted it when he winked at her. She stood up. "You need to report this to Captain Guerrero."

Will's shoulders slumped, but he didn't look miserable anymore. He nodded. "Right. I'll do that now." He left.

She moved around the table to sit next to Erikson. "That's one mystery solved."

"You're burying the lede." Erickson rested his elbows on the table and propped his chin on his folded hands. "You like me. You really like me."

Shelby was saved from responding when Naomi tore into the conference room.

"Detectives, I'm having the hotel security email you the footage now."

Shelby grabbed her laptop from the table. She, Erickson, and Naomi crowded around it in the conference room. As soon as her email pinged with a new message, Shelby clicked open the email. Two videos were attached, one for that Friday night, and one for Saturday morning. She opened the video for Friday night, noting the parking garage only had one entrance and exit. The camera captured cars as they passed through the gate.

"Officer Kim, what kind of car does Principal Wheeler drive?" Shelby fast-forwarded the video.

Naomi chewed her bottom lip, thinking. "A maroon Honda Accord, four-door."

Shelby paused the video every time a reddish sedan exited the garage. Finally, at 10:35 p.m., a maroon Honda Accord pulled up to the gate. She played the video at regular speed. A wave of excitement burned along her nerve endings as she watched Alfred Wheeler lean out of his car to pay for parking at the kiosk. If the principal left Pittsburgh at 10:35 p.m., he had enough time to drive back to Locust Grove, wait for Whitney at the pool, and strangle her.

"Got him." She turned to Naomi, whose face had gone slack. "Officer Kim, put out an APB on Principal Wheeler." Naomi swallowed, nodded, and scurried back to her desk.

When Shelby turned back to her laptop, Erickson was speeding through Saturday's video. He said, "Just want to double-check."

The gate was much busier on Saturday morning than Friday night. While Erickson watched the video, Shelby pulled a file from the stack on the conference table. "Tom Long drives a white Dodge caravan." Erickson nodded. A few minutes after ten a.m., a white Dodge caravan stopped at the gate. Erickson paused the video and grinned at Shelby. "At least that part of the timeline was true."

They jumped out of their seats, throwing on their jackets, and grabbing their gear. Shelby pulled up Wheeler's home address as they walked out of the station toward her car. She turned on her red-and-blues, but left off the siren. She didn't want to scare Wheeler away if he was home.

Erickson drummed a beat on the dashboard as she pulled onto the street. "We're coming for you, teddy bear."

Thirty-Four

Shelby maneuvered around cars and through intersections, the red-and-blues flashing on top of her car. The sky had darkened, and clouds had gathered while they'd been in the station. A heavy rain would hinder their search. Shelby hoped the bad weather would hold off.

"He's got two kids at home." Erickson gripped the handle above the passenger seat. "He can't just take off to parts unknown, right?"

"Maybe. Maybe not. His son is eighteen. Wheeler could make him a guardian of his daughter to cover his ass."

"I don't think he expected to get caught. I know he didn't count on Tom Long ratting him out."

"And there's one more thing." She barreled through an intersection, tires squealing as other drivers skidded to a stop.

Erickson gripped the handle above his head. "What"?

Shelby swung around the last bend before stopping in front of Wheeler's house. "Those red jerseys hanging in his office."

She strode to the front door while Erickson checked the garage. She rang the doorbell, then knocked hard enough to shake the storm door. Erickson joined her. "Car's gone." She nodded, expecting as much.

The door swung open. A tall, skinny boy eyed them, a crease between his brows. His shoulders were wide, like his father's, but he lacked the muscle that came with maturity. "Hi?"

"Is your father home?" Shelby asked.

His eyes widened and bounced between the detectives. "No. He just left. Is he in trouble?"

Erickson stepped forward. "What makes you say that?"

The boy crossed his arms and chewed on his chapped bottom lip. "He was acting all weird. Like, he ran around packing like he was in a race or something. Told me he had a school emergency and would be gone for a few days." He shook his head. "A school emergency? So basic."

"Did he say where he was going?" Shelby asked, her stomach plummeting to the ground.

"Nah. Just said he'd call us tonight. What's going on?"

Erickson pulled a business card out of his wallet. "If your dad comes home or calls, call me at this number."

When the teen saw the police logo on the card, he stepped back from the door. "You're the cops? I thought you were parents with a beef." His face paled. "Is this about Whitney?"

Shelby and Erickson were already walking toward Shelby's car. Erickson called over his shoulder, "Just call me if your father gets in touch." Erickson hopped in the car, shaking his head. "Never meet your heroes."

Shelby made a U-turn and drove toward the main road. "There's one highway out of town. Fifty-fifty shot at which way he went. Suggestions?"

Erickson, hand on the grab handle again, said, "A lot more places to hide in Pittsburgh than anywhere south of here. Easier to get lost in the crowd."

"North it is."

Shelby hit the siren along with the lights, just as the first heavy drops of rain splattered onto her windshield. She turned on her wipers as she swerved around cars. She hit the entrance ramp to the highway at top speed, pressing her foot to the Toyota's floor, driving as fast as she could without flipping the SUV or hydroplaning.

She craned her neck as they came to a hill. "There's a maroon sedan, about a quarter mile ahead. Pull up Wheeler's license plate." She dodged between cars, cursing when drivers were slow to pull off to the side, even for a police siren.

Erickson tapped the screen mounted on Shelby's dashboard. "Got it."

When she was a handful of cars away from the maroon sedan, it jumped forward in a burst of speed.

"That's him. He's running." She gave her Toyota more gas. The rain slammed her windshield.

Erickson had to raise his voice above the rain's drumming. "He's going to get someone killed if he doesn't stop."

Shelby whispered a prayer for herself and Erickson, for the people on the road, and for Wheeler.

An exit ramp came into view. From the angle of Wheeler's car, Shelby realized he was heading in that direction.

Erickson noticed, too. "There's nothing off this ramp but trees and homes. Please tell me he won't make us chase him on some pot-holed one-lane road."

Wheeler's car slowed the tiniest bit to take the exit ramp. He cut off a small hatchback that swerved toward the berm, then bounced back onto the highway, horn blaring as Wheeler fishtailed up the ramp. "Jesus," Shelby breathed. "You're right. He's going to kill someone."

The exit ramp climbed a steep hill. A stop sign waited for Wheeler at the top of the slope, where he could turn left or right. On the opposite side of the intersection, the ridge fell away, just a straight drop-off. Wheeler ignored the stop sign and turned left at top speed. The detectives watched in horror as his car spun out on the wet road, sliding away from them. It fell over the ridge, vanishing from view.

A sheet of rain filled Shelby's view. Her windshield wipers showed her Wheeler's disappearance frame by frame, almost in slow motion. In her mind, she already pictured the ambulance, the stretcher, the body covered by a sheet. She already knew their day would be long, exhausting, and, depending on what they found at the bottom of that ridge, a nightmare.

Shelby slowed to a stop, parking near the stop sign. She turned off the siren, but left her lights on to warn oncoming cars of possible danger.

The detectives jumped out of the car, firearms drawn, and approached the edge of the road above the drop-off. Shelby blinked against the rain. The Honda, crunched and crumpled, rested at the bottom of the hill on its wheels, steam and smoke escaping from the hood, the headlights dimmed by tall grass. Wheeler appeared to be slumped at the wheel.

Now soaking wet, they went as quickly as they could down the steep, slippery slope, feet sideways, finding purchase on grass clumps and rocks. Ten feet away from the car, they pointed their weapons at Wheeler, who was still bent forward against the exploded air bag.

"Alfred Wheeler, you're under arrest." Shelby called as she crept forward. "Put your hands where we can see them." The sound of the rain hitting the roof mixed with the engine's hissing and clunking. They moved closer. The driver's side window was splintered, but intact. Wheeler groaned, then touched his face. His hand came away covered in blood.

"Wheeler," Erickson shouted. "Get out of the car and put your hands up."

The principal didn't move, didn't acknowledge the detectives. Just as Shelby reached for the door, Wheeler's shoulders shook. She stepped back quickly. Wheeler lifted his head, leaned back against the headrest, and wailed.

Erickson shot Shelby a look that said, "What the hell?"

She pressed her lips together and approached the door again. She holstered her weapon, but threw Erickson a look, letting him know to cover her. He nodded. Shelby gripped the door handle with both hands. Bracing her right foot against the car, she could wrench the door open. Metal on metal shrieked. Wheeler's sobbing filled the field. Although blood streamed from his nose, and purple bruises bloomed around his eyes, he seemed to be in one piece.

"Alfred Wheeler," Shelby began again, "you're under arrest for the murder of Whitney Chandler." She continued giving his Miranda rights, finishing with, "Do you understand the rights I have just read to you?" Wheeler dropped his head forward, barely nodding.

"Out loud, Wheeler." Erickson had joined Shelby at the side of the car.

"Yes," Wheeler howled.

"Get out, hands up." Erickson holstered his weapon, too. Alfred Wheeler looked like all the fight had drained out of him on his roll down the hill.

While Erickson handcuffed Wheeler, shoving him against the car with slightly more force than was necessary, Shelby inspected the car. It was dented and folded in places, but the interior was in surprisingly good shape. The back seat was empty, so she moved to the trunk. Unfortunately, it was smashed inward; the lid wedged under the bumper.

"Wait here," Shelby said. While Erickson called in the arrest, she climbed the hill, slipping here and there on wet grass and mud. She retrieved a crowbar from her car and clambered back down the hill. When she walked toward the Honda's trunk, Wheeler started weeping again. Erickson, holding Wheeler against the car, rolled his eyes. She jammed the crowbar between the trunk's lid and the bumper, then leaned all her weight on it. The locking mechanism popped off, and the trunk sprung free. She lifted the lid and stared at the contents, still intact. Wheeler's suitcase and a large, green garbage bag. She slipped on a pair of nitrile gloves from her pocket and dumped out the garbage bag. Out fell a framed Bobcats jersey and a purse. She reached into the purse and pulled out a cellphone.

Erickson lifted his eyebrows. She nodded. They caught Whitney's killer.

"After we take in this piece of shit," Erickson said, "margaritas are on me."

Thirty-Five

"Not too tough for a drug kingpin," Erickson said while he eyed Principal Wheeler through the two-way mirror. "Or prepared. Doesn't seem like he had any plan at all for getting caught. Not even a lawyer on retainer. No game. No poker face. Guess he really is a teddy bear."

Shelby shrugged. "He's obviously an amateur. Just wanted to make some extra money." She heaved a sigh. "I wish they'd never made *Breaking Bad*."

Erickson gave her a startled look, then threw back his head and laughed. She hadn't meant it as a joke, but seeing Erickson losing it made her realize how ridiculous she'd sounded. She chuckled, too, giddy now that the adrenaline of the chase was wearing off. Her muscles ached and fatigue pulled at her like an undertow. They'd changed into the spare clothes they kept in their lockers. Shelby's damp hair was pulled back into a low ponytail, while Erickson's was stylishly finger combed. She rolled her shoulders back. "Let's get some answers."

She led Erickson into the interrogation room, where Wheeler sat slumped like he had in his car. Gone was his usual affability. Tears leaked from his swollen eyes. His clothes were rumpled and blood-stained. He wrung his cuffed hands on the tabletop. He didn't lift his eyes until the detectives were seated.

Shelby hit a button on a small remote to begin recording their session, giving the date, time, and other details. Then she said, "Mr. Wheeler, tell us about Friday night."

His expression was sullen as he met Shelby's eyes. "Should I call a lawyer?" His head fell back. "What's the point? What do you want to know?"

Erickson said, "Let's start with you leaving the hotel in Pittsburgh. You originally told us you came home Saturday morning."

"But that wasn't true," Shelby added. "You left Pittsburgh around ten-thirty p.m. Friday night. Where did you go?"

Wheeler stared at his hands, picking at the nail on his forefinger with his thumb. "I came back to Locust Grove."

"Where specifically?" Erickson asked.

Wheeler swallowed. "Bianchi's. The pool."

"Why did you go to an empty pool?" Erickson's voice was light, but his eyes were predatory.

Wheeler looked at him. "To meet Whitney Chandler." He closed his lips on a sob.

"Mr. Wheeler," Shelby said, "don't make us pull this out of you one question at a time. It will go better for you if you just tell us everything that happened. The whole truth. Leave nothing out."

Wheeler nodded and swallowed. "Yeah, okay. It doesn't matter now, anyway, does it?" His watery blue eyes found Shelby's. She waited for him to continue, but he said, "Do you know how much college costs? Not for an Ivy League school or some fancy private school. Any college. It's goddam expensive." Shelby narrowed her eyes while Erickson leaned back in his chair and crossed his arms. "Tuition and room and board are astronomical. You pray your kid gets a scholarship. But my kids? They're not getting scholarships." He moved to run a hand through his hair, but the cuffs didn't reach that far. He went back to picking his nails. "Hannah plays soccer, but she's not good enough for a full ride." He grimaced. "My son is smart, but not a genius. Do you know what a genius you have to be to get an academic scholarship?"

He shook his head. "We need financial aid, but I make just enough not to qualify."

Erickson raised an eyebrow. "So, selling drugs was the answer? Your wife can't chip in? What about your kids getting jobs?"

Wheeler's eyes snapped to Erickson's. "My children will not work jobs like some welfare family." Erickson scoffed. "As for my wife," Wheeler shook his head, "she has her own student debt to pay off. She can chip in a little, but not nearly enough."

"So," Erickson said, "drugs."

"Oh, get off your high horse. You wait until you have kids. You'll be amazed at what you're willing to do to give them a better life than you had."

Erickson, arms still crossed, shrugged. "My dad was a farmer. Cops don't make much. I'm not rich, but you won't see me selling drugs, that's for damn sure."

Shelby held out a placating hand. "Back to Friday night. You went to the pool to meet Whitney. Why?"

Wheeler pulled his eyes away from Erickson's, staring at his hands again. "She said she wanted to talk about her cut. She'd been bugging me for weeks for more money, saying she and the other kids were the ones doing the work. That they deserved a bigger percentage because I was just the supplier." He shook his head. "Ridiculous. And stupid. She was book smart, but had no common sense."

"Other kids? How many?"

"Five or six at a time, depending on who needs money."

Erickson rested his forearms on the table. "We'll need names before we're finished."

Wheeler nodded. "In her last text, she threatened me. Said I'd better be ready to renegotiate, or she wouldn't keep her mouth shut anymore." He looked up with imploring eyes. "I'm the goddam principal. I couldn't have her telling her parents what we were doing, or worse, going to the police." He acted as if they sympathized.

Shelby wondered if he'd thought about how badly his reputation would suffer after going to prison for murder. "So, you met her at the pool?"

"Yeah. She set the place and time. Said no one would see us there."

"You wore gloves," Erickson said.

Wheeler nodded. "And the jersey."

Shelby said, "To implicate Bobby."

Wheeler nodded. "He's already got a reputation for violence, on and off the field. And he's big. I knew everyone would think he did it."

"Except," Erickson said, "he had an alibi."

"What?" Wheeler chuckled. "Being at home in bed? I didn't think you'd believe him."

Shane had kept Wheeler well-informed if he knew Bobby's alibi.

"No." Shelby laced her fingers together on the table. "As it turns out, Del Coleman verified Bobby's whereabouts when Whitney was killed. He had a solid alibi." Wheeler shook his head in disgust, like Del Coleman had personally wronged him by not going along with his plan. "You wore the jersey to implicate Bobby. Then returned the jersey to its frame? Why not just wear a fan jersey?"

"I was in a hurry." Wheeler spread his hands. "You have to pre-order those, so I grabbed the closest one."

"Then returned it to the frame afterwards," Erickson said. "Where no one would think to look."

Wheeler smirked. "Turned out grabbing the nearest jersey was the smartest thing I could do. It was hiding in plain sight when you two visited me."

The arrogance of killers never ceased to astound Shelby. Wheeler was bragging about hiding evidence while sitting in an interrogation room in handcuffs. "Out of curiosity, did you send Whitney a mum for homecoming?" Mum's the word.

Wheeler's eyebrows pinched together. "Yeah, trying to shut her up. How did you know that?"

She shook her head. "Not important." Another nail in his coffin. "So, Shelby arrives at what time?"

"Midnight."

"What happened then?"

He rolled his eyes. "She threatened me again, but got more specific. Said she wouldn't bother telling her parents. She'd go straight to the police. And she pointed out that as a straight-A student, they were likely to believe her. She said they'd let her go for turning me in." He pressed his lips together. "That was all I could take."

"What do you mean? What happened?" Erickson said, his eyes laser-focused on Wheeler.

Finally, Wheeler appeared remorseful. "I strangled her. I was just so angry. She wouldn't stop..." He swallowed. "I just wanted to stop her. I didn't realize how final it would be."

"Yeah," Erickson sighed. "Death's kinda funny like that." Wheeler's eyes took on a shine. "So, Whitney's dead. Then what?"

Wheeler gathered himself. "I stood there for a while, a few minutes. She was so still." He shook his head. "Then I grabbed her purse and her phone, just in case she had something on me."

"What about the clothes you wore that night? The gloves? Your shoes?" Shelby said.

"I burned them in our backyard fire pit and threw the ashes in the trash."

Shelby glanced at Erickson. They'd have to retrieve the ashes from Wheeler's garbage to see if they could salvage anything.

"Where did you go after you left the pool?"

"Home." He shrugged. "My kids were still asleep. I knew I'd be up before them. They didn't know I'd left the hotel early. They just figured I came home Saturday morning."

"And the brick?"

Wheeler's eyes shot wide with surprise. Again, he tried to run his hand through his hair and failed. "Yeah, that was me. I took one from our fire pit."

"I'll send you the bill for my front window." She narrowed her eyes at Wheeler. "Were you trying to keep us focused on Bobby?"

"Yes," Wheeler mumbled.

Erickson snickered. "And you thought a note tied to a brick would be enough for us to arrest him?"

"It worked, didn't it?" Wheeler's mouth tilted sideways. "You arrested him."

"Um, who's sitting here? You or Bobby?"

That sobered Wheeler. He looked at them with bloodshot eyes. "What happens now?"

Thirty-Six

Sunlight bounced off the ice in the golden margaritas that sat in front of Shelby and Erickson. The fall day was unseasonably warm, giving the outdoor dining area at Fiesta Mexican Grill the feel of summer. The murmur of other diners and the clinks of cutlery on plates formed a soothing background to a relaxing lunch.

Erickson lifted his drink, the yellow lenses of his polarized Ray-Bans shading his eyes. "To us and our unparalleled brilliance."

Shelby laughed, her light brown hair swinging around her shoulders. "I don't know about that. How about, to a well-earned day off?"

"Hell, yeah. I'll drink to that." They each sipped from the salted rims of their glasses.

Their food arrived. A simple fish taco platter for Shelby, and sizzling steak fajitas for Erickson, for which he applauded, causing a bit of a scene. Shelby shook her head and bit into a taco. "Back to Brooke County for you?"

Erickson wrapped grilled steak and veggies into a fajita. "Yep." He held up his hand. "Please, dry those eyes, Reed. I'm only a phone call away."

She dabbed at her mouth with a napkin, chuckling. "Look, I'm reluctant to admit this, but—"

"You've fallen madly in love with me. Can't live without me." He whipped the sunglasses from his face and sang. "Here we stand, worlds apart, hearts broken in two—"

Shelby laughed and grabbed his wrist. "Stop." He broke off the song and grinned. "Were you drinking before I got here?"

"Nah, just high on life. I told you; I needed this win." He grew serious for a moment, meeting her gaze. "You were saying?" He bit into his fajita.

"I was saying," she looked at her plate, "that I'm reluctant to admit this, but I really enjoyed having you as a partner." She met his eyes. "We worked well together."

He gave her a small smile, the corners of his eyes crinkling. "We did, Detective Reed."

Her phone buzzed next to her plate. She glanced at it and read her father's text before it vanished.

Dad: Proud of you.

She hated how much his words meant to her. The only thing keeping her from tearing up was catching Erickson watching her in her peripheral vision. She looked up, and he raised his eyebrows in question. She said, "Just another political message."

He rolled his eyes before returning his attention to his fajita.

They ate in companionable silence for a minute, then Erickson said, "I think I'm going to look into volunteering as a football coach at the high school next year."

Shelby's eyes widened. "That's quite a commitment, especially with your schedule."

He shrugged. "Hopefully, the thieves, drug dealers, and spousal abusers can find some Zen during the fall." He winked at her. She pressed her lips together to keep from smiling. "Even if I can't commit to them fully, I want to be involved." His eyes roamed the patio. "After talking to Bobby and Del, how they felt they had to hide themselves from the world," he shook his head and brought his gaze back to Shelby. "I want to help kids like that. I want to show them they shouldn't feel ashamed. And I want the other kids to know it's not okay to bully someone just because they're different. You know?" He took another bite.

She nodded. "I know." Erickson had more depth than she had realized when they met. A burst of warmth for him filled her chest, something she hadn't felt in a long time. "Good for you."

He bowed his head. "Thanks." He winked again. "I know I'm awesome. I have the mug to prove it."

She chuckled, holding her napkin over her mouth. Erickson made life seem so easy. He saw a need and filled it. Silver linings were everywhere for him. Shelby hoped one day she could be so relaxed, to take each day in stride.

Watching Erickson devour his fajita, she put down her taco and took a fortifying drink from her margarita. She sucked in a breath. "My husband was murdered." She kept her eyes on her plate. Erickson stilled, his fajita halfway to his mouth. "Right on our doorstep." She raised her eyes to his. "And it was because of me."

Erickson put down his food, his eyebrows pulling together. "What do you mean?"

She took another deep breath. "I don't like to talk about it. It's so painful." She rested her fist on her sternum.

"Maybe that's why it's so painful." He folded his arms on the table. "Because you don't talk about it."

She frowned. "Maybe." She swallowed. "About five years ago, I was working on a case. It was horrific." She dragged her fork through her refried beans. "Do you remember the Davante Johnson case?"

Erickson rubbed his chin, then said, "The kid from Harrisburg who raped a girl at a party?"

She gave a slow nod. "Yeah."

"Shit." He leaned back. "That was your case?" When she nodded again, he said, "That was all over national news. It was a huge story." Then he remembered and closed his eyes. "Your husband. Davante shot him when he answered the door." His head dropped, and he ran his fingers through his hair. Then he met her gaze with eyes full of sympathy and sorrow. "My God, Shelby. I didn't realize. I didn't put it together." He ran his hand over his jaw. "Five years ago, I was helping my parents split up their farm and sell it. I had zero focus left for anything other than that and my job. Shelby, I'm so sorry. I didn't know."

She shrugged. "Why would you? I kept my maiden name. My husband's name was Ingram. Shawn Ingram." She put down her fork. "The girl's name was Alison Shepard. She and her friends went to an after-game party for the Stanton Stampede."

"The football team."

"Right. They got drunk. Very drunk. So did the players."

His jaw ticked. "Hormones and alcohol. Not a great combo."

"No. And the girls didn't know that the players had a secret initiation. Usually choosing one girl—a virgin, not that it matters—and one player." She gritted her teeth.

Erickson shook his head like he was shaking images from his mind. "Jesus."

"Anyway, it was ugly. Getting anyone to talk was excruciating. The parents and the school were nightmares. They suspected what had happened and wanted nothing more than to throw me off the case. They wanted to protect the boys, the school's reputation. Same old story. Then I finally broke through to one boy and the rest fell like dominos. It was heartbreaking and exhausting." She took a sip of her margarita. "I had enough to convict Davante. No question. I arrested him, but no one thought he was a flight risk. The judge set a low bail and—" She shared a sad smile. "The school's booster club paid."

Erickson reached across the table and took Shelby's hand. A week ago, she would have pulled away. But she knew Erickson's offer of friendship was sincere. And it was time to let people in again.

"It was a gorgeous fall day, a lot like this one." She raised her face to the sun, closing her eyes for a moment. "I was out, running errands. I pulled into the driveway just as Davante ran away." She sniffed back tears, blinking. "I ran to the front door, but Shawn was already fading." Her lips trembled. "I told him I loved him." She held Erickson's eyes, wet with unshed tears. "We got to say goodbye."

Erickson cleared his throat. "Why Shawn?"

Shelby pulled her hand from Erickson's and wiped her eyes, sitting back. "He meant to shoot me. But he was so angry he wasn't thinking. He fired as soon as Shawn opened the door."

"Shelby, I'm so sorry."

"Thank you." A lightness spread through Shelby, as if someone lifted a heavy beam from her chest and freed her. "Thank you for listening. Maybe I should talk about it more."

His head tilted. "That's why you were so hesitant to blame Bobby. It must have felt like you were reliving it all over again."

"A little." She ran her finger through the condensation on the side of her glass. "At the trial, Davante said I had ruined his life." She wiped her finger on the tablecloth. "But Shawn paid the price." Erickson opened his mouth, but Shelby stopped him. "I know that's not true. But it brought home the responsibility we have not to ruin someone's life if they're innocent. We're so focused on arresting people and closing cases that sometimes the guilty ones slip away while the innocent end up behind bars. It's a perspective I hadn't considered well enough until then."

Erickson stared at her. "You're right. I hadn't thought about it that way. Still," he sighed, "I'm sorry that happened." He shared a sad smile. "I admire you, Shelby. A lot of people would have quit."

"It had the opposite effect. I wanted to do better."

"Well, I certainly saw that on this case." He lifted his glass. "To Shelby Reed." He winked, lightening the mood.

She rolled her eyes. "I'm not toasting myself."

"All right." He placed his forefinger on his lips, pretending to think. Then he lifted his glass again. "To doing better."

She smiled. For the first time in years, her future looked bigger, brighter. She lifted her glass. "To doing better."

They emptied their glasses.

Erickson smacked his lips and squinted. "I wonder what they have for dessert?"

The End

* * *

Thank you for reading Bright Girl! If you liked this mystery, please consider leaving a rating and/or a review.

Exclusive bonus chapter! Find out what happened at the Locust Grove police station the night Erickson wrote the report without Shelby's approval. Read a bonus chapter of that evening from Erickson's point-of-view. Go to https://short.im/free-bgbonus to download it now!

Acknowledgement

Thanks to Jeff McGowan for his forensic expertise and input. Special thanks to Brienne Brown for her editing skills and positive feedback. As always, thank you to Ross, my husband. I couldn't do it without you.

Books by this Author

Roadside Homicide

The first book in the River Sutton Mysteries. Robin returns home for her sister's wedding, only to stumble onto a murder with deep secrets. Small town, second chance romance, cozy mystery.

A Fatal Fumble River Sutton Mysteries, Book 2

It's fall, y'all. Robin returns home for her high school's 100th homecoming football game, only to become the prime suspect in her former frenemy's murder. Small town, second chance romance, cozy mystery.

Jingle Bell Justice River Sutton Mysteries, Book 3

Jenn and Deb open their own B&B. But the murder of a socialite turns their dream into a nightmare. Robin has to uncover the killer to save Deb. Small town, clean romance, cozy mystery.

The Haunting of Ivy May

A paranormal cozy mystery! Ivy May is looking for a new beginning after her divorce. But the Victorian fixer-upper she bought for a song has a ghostly resident who is reluctant to leave. How will she kick this ghost to the curb while fending off her ex? Small town, clean romance.

Go to https://www.nancy-basile.com to find these books and more.

Award-winning author Nancy Basile grew up in the hills of West Virginia, scraping her knees, and dreaming about becoming a murder mystery writer. Now, she's bringing West Virginia to life in the pages of her mysteries. Her second book in the River Sutton Mysteries, "A Fatal Fumble," won BookFest's LGBTQ+ Mystery Award, and took 2nd place for both Cozy Mystery and Amateur Sleuth. Although she lives in Amish Country, Pennsylvania with her husband and two children, she'll always be a West Virginia girl at heart. Find out more about Nancy's books and sign up for her newsletter at https://www.nancy-basile.com